John N. King
Johnnk1996@aol.com
202-360-6508

Of Scales and Fur – Rocket
By: John N. King
Approx.: 37,000 words

Table of Contents

Dedicated to my family and to the writers of the Write Practice.

Thank you all for your unending support and love.

As the red dragon, Rocket stepped into the antechamber beside the throne room, she gazed at Connors - the King of Humans - in curiosity. Though the dragons defended humanity from any and all supernatural threats, it was still rare for the King of Humans himself to ask for a personal visit.

However, it quickly came together when Connors held up a photo. A photo Rocket recognized.

The man was sticking his tongue out at the camera, his hazel eyes winking with irreverent mischief. His jet-black hair was stuck up in a fauxhawk style, and a loud tropical shirt glowed at the bottom of the picture. His most striking feature, however, was the scar, stretching from his lower lip to the top of his ear, pulling his face into a permanent, distorted smirk.

"Lucas Cooper," Connors explained. "He always calls himself 'Luco.'" He leaned back, letting the shadows mix with his black robe, blending him into darkness. "For a time, we thought that he was a friend and ally: he had knowledge of the occult and magic, and used it to help General Drake create... well... you."

He looked at Rocket's draconic visage: her large, leathery wings, her cherry-red scales glittering, and her powerful tail swinging from side to side. Her electric green eyes glittered, the pupils contracting to slits.

"Sounds like I owe him a lot," she mused.

Connors hummed, his hood failing to conceal his smirk. "Normally." His smile faded. "But then we discovered the truth."

He tossed another picture next to Luco's. At first it appeared to be a wolf, except that it stood on two legs, and its front paws were actually human hands, topped with razor sharp claws. Its gold eyes shone with eerie intelligence befitting that of a human, and a mane of dreadlocked hair pieces flowed from the back of its head. A white mask covered most of the wolf's snout.

Rocket growled at the white mask. "Myst," she snarled, before looking up at Connors. "You can't tell me Luco's involved with Myst, right? She's been killing people like him for the past ten years. She's the reason I'm here; so I can protect you from her and her army of demi-wolf freaks!"

"Indeed," Connors agreed. "But Luco's the one that created her. And then set her on the path of murder in the first place by conditioning her to hate humans."

Rocket stiffened, but Connors just laughed.

"Oh, don't act so surprised, my dear. Shiva showed you the truth far before I did, did she not?"

Rocket snorted. "And you expect me to trust that dog?" She looked away, glowering as she remembered Shiva. That snow-white fur; those chocolate brown eyes that tried so hard to look innocent and meek. But Rocket knew better. "Myst created her; gave her that freaky 'Pack Link' thing that lets her read minds and force lies into my head." Her fist clenched as she remembered the eerie glowing tendrils emanating from Shiva's body. "She killed my Rider."

Connors' eyes flashed with anger from under his hood. "And as we've discussed, your Rider struck first. Shiva acted in self-defense. According to my research, Luco did the same thing with Myst." He raised a hand just before Rocket could snarl. "However, I will not deny; Myst took it too far when she turned her rage on those who didn't deserve it."

Rocket sighed and leaned back. "So, what's the plan?" she asked. "How are we dealing with Myst and Luco?"

Connors smiled. "Shiva has taken care of Myst; regardless of whether you trust her or not, the white demi-wolf has managed to keep Myst contained in White Fang Wood for the past year." His smile faded. "That being said, my scouts have noticed Luco patrolling the edge of the wolves' territory. I'm concerned he's looking re-ignite the war between dragons and demi-wolves. He has to be stopped."

Rocket grimaced. "And why me?" she asked. "Why not Bang or Cinder?" She looked down as her voice grew solemn. "Those are dragons who know how to protect their Riders."

Connors laid a hand on her talon in empathy. "You did everything you could," he assured her. "It wasn't your fault." He grinned. "Besides, since you're currently without a Rider, it's got me thinking… how does General Drake handle dragons who lose their Riders?"

Rocket flinched, thinking back to the General; an imposing tower of a man with brown eyes marbled with flecks of gold and red, making it look like he had literal fire for eyes.

"He… finds us a replacement. We can't exactly sit on the sidelines if we're needed." She tilted her head. "Why do you ask?"

"Because even though you claim to hate Shiva," Connors said. "I know that you saw the good in her. You took pity on her when she was lost and alone and adjusting to her new life."

Rocket glowered. "And my pity got my Rider killed."

"That's not true, Rocket. Let's not go into that again." Connors leaned forward. "You've seen enough to not be so naïve; you can no longer assume that all demi-wolves are evil and all humans are good. Luco is not good. He is an anarchist and a psychopath who is willing to let dozens of humans, dragons and wolves be killed for his own sick entertainment."

Rocket crossed her arms, but didn't refute the King. Until…

"Shiva never wanted the war, and has genuinely sought peace. You need to recognize that the enemy of your enemy is your friend. Can you understand that?"

A long moment stretched between them as she pondered what he had said. It was true; the enemy of her enemy was her friend. But the wolves? After everything they had done under Myst's reign? It clashed with everything Rocket was taught. Shiva was one thing, but Myst or any of the other wolves… they were something else.

Connors grimaced, no doubt sensing that it was going to be a hard sell. Rocket prided herself on being stubborn, to be sure. But, the King pushed forward and spoke.

"Rocket. I want you to take a wolf as your new Rider."

Rocket's reaction was immediate and visceral. "No," she growled impertinently, forgetting who she was talking to.

But the King's countenance was stone. "Rocket…"

"NO!" she boomed. "Sir, you know I can't work with one of them!"

"Ignis-Drake R065!" King Connors barked.

Rocket seethed, but swallowed the flames in her throat.

"I understand this is difficult for you," the King said.

"Your Majesty," she asked. "May I have some time to think about this?"

He nodded. "Take some time, but let's keep this between us. You're dismissed."

Rocket managed a small bow, then swept out of the room.

Chapter 1 – Rocket

Rocket should have known something was off. As she followed the trail of jet-like smoke that led to Luco's mount Blaze, she could feel a nagging foreboding in her mind, alerting her of treachery and deceit.

However, Rocket's anger was deep and seething, and blinded her to her intuition.

Her grief over the death of Buck – her rider – still hung like a great weight on her heart. As she passed the borders to White Fang Wood, she noticed the furry bodies of the demi-wolves lurking in the shadows of the trees, and resisted the urge to shoot flames at them. It all started with them, after all. Them and their twisted Alpha, Myst. Trying to tear down human society, stealing dogs to mutate into more demi-wolves.

"No one has been able to stop her," Drake told Rocket. *"But you, my little Rocket, you're finally going to bring an end to her reign of terror."*

That had been the mission. Stop Myst and protect humanity. For most of her life, that had been her goal. That was what she was bred to do. Defend the innocent.

But then, she learned the truth. All along, Myst was the pawn of an even greater threat: Luco. One of the very humans Rocket was created to protect, and yet he generated a monster, resulting in the deaths of thousands of people. Why?

'Because I can.' His mocking voice said– even in a memory that could've been false – and it made her inner fire simmer with rage. *'Because who's going to stop me?'*

Rocket wanted stop him. She thought she was ready to show him that although he, too, was human, it didn't give him the right to let others suffer for his own amusement.

Yet, as she caught sight of her target, she found her resolve faltering. Luco was in a modest village. There was a school, a marketplace and a few other buildings where adults walked back and forth carrying goods, and children played near the school. Luco himself sauntered along with a baseball bat perched on his shoulder like an umbrella, deep in conversation with a young man wringing his hands and nodding to whatever Luco was saying. Luco's yellow dragon Blaze meandered along behind them, stifling a smile as the children chased after her tail.

Rocket unconsciously began to smile at the scene of domestic tranquility that was at complete odds with what she had anticipated. Blaze let one child seize her tail before lifting him into the air. The little human screeched with delight as he rose into the air and fell, before Blaze caught him and gently set him down. The child let go and ran back to his friends laughing with delight, while another stepped forward to grab Blaze's tail and took a ride as well.

But Rocket couldn't focus on the children for too long. As she descended, the human adults pointed and whispered in awe. Their whispering drew Luco's gaze, and the rider's distorted grin widened as he stepped forward to greet Rocket.

"Rocky," he called, as she landed before him. "Good to see you, my friend."

Blaze looked up, her pink eyes widening in delight. She gave Rocket a salute. For a moment, the rider and his yellow mount paused, their eyes darting to Rocket's back.

"Where's your Rider?" Luco asked.

Rocket's smile vanished, struggling to ignore the flare of guilt and grief that shot into her heart. "You know what happened to him."

Luco's grin faded as he remembered. He nodded solemnly, stretching his back. "Ah, yes… Indeed." He looked to his human companion. "Apologies, Mr. Walker, if you'll excuse me for a moment."

"Oh, uh… sure, yeah. Okay," Mr. Walker replied, stepping back as Luco motioned for Rocket to follow. Together, the two walked between two merchant stands to the outskirts of the village, away from any onlookers. Blaze stayed behind, continuing to play with the children.

"It's a terrible thing, to lose a man like that," Luco noted. "He was a powerful fighter." He chuckled. "Then again, you have to be to ride a dragon, yeah?"

Rocket nodded, doubt bubbling in her gut. Was this really the man she was supposed to defeat? A man whose dragon was a friend to children? A man who at least demonstrated some sympathy for her loss? Connors had warned her that not all humans were good, and yet… Rocket couldn't help but doubt him.

"Myst will tell you that the humans are evil," Drake had told her. *"That they don't deserve this world. She's wrong; humans have good in them. And that good is worth protecting."*

"So," Luco's voice snapped her out of her thoughts. "What brings you here?" He grinned at Blaze, who was still entertaining the kids. "Here to see your sister?" His eyes grew crafty. "Or is the King taking an interest in my activities?"

Rocket was hesitant. This conversation was not what she had anticipated. "He says that you've been… 'involved' with the creation of the wolves."

Luco hummed. "Has he now?" He chuckled. "So, he believes that white dog?"

Rocket, who's hatred of Myst was as deep as any, didn't know how to answer. "Well… you're not involved with their creation right? Shiva was just lying! Using… tricks or something."

In her heart, she found herself wanting it to not be true. This was all some kind of mistake.

Luco's laugh was so warm, that for a moment, Rocket dared to hope that the King had been mistaken. Humans weren't bad, after all. They…

"Oh, my dear dragon," Luco cooed. "You should know by now… wolves can be vicious and cruel…" His grin widened at Rocket's sigh of relief. "But they are far from liars."

Rocket's heart dropped into her stomach; her grin faded away. "W-What?"

Luco chuckled at her confusion. "How does it feel?" he mused. "Having your entire worldview crumble down around you? Learning that everything you've fought for was nothing but a lie?"

He turned away as if to only look at the countryside, leaving himself exposed; undefended. Rocket, meanwhile, blinked, frozen in disbelief.

"W-What are you talking about?" she stammered. "Y-You're not…! But you're human! A human wouldn't…"

Luco's laugh turned cold. "You still can't see it?" he mused over his shoulder. "Well, I suppose it makes some sense. Your faith in my kind is not completely misplaced. We can be kind. We can be patient. Heck, you and Blaze can say that we're quite good masters." His voice turned cruel. "But give us too much power; let us have too much control… and we'll start thinking that the world is ours to do with as we please."

Rocket shook her head. "A-Are you being serious, Luco?"

The man turned back to her, continuing to roll the baseball bat over his shoulder. "Of course, you don't realize it at first. Like Myst. You won't believe how long she clung to her fleeting hope. The amount of time it took me to beat out any sympathy she had for humans?" His fingers tightened on the bat. "I wasn't able to lift my arms for a week."

He laughed, as Rocket's scales glowed; disbelief turning to rage. He leaned in.

"But it was worth it," Luco whispered, spreading his arms out to the countryside like he wanted to hug it. "She did better than I could have hoped for. And when Drake sent you – his guardians, his honest souls?" He chuckled. "The battles were glorious!"

"The battles were sick!" Rocket hissed, struggling to hold back her flames. "People died! My Rider died!"

Luco's eyes glittered with cruelty. "Then I guess he wasn't worth his salt as a fighter."

In Rocket's mind, she saw the conversation with Connors. She thought, *you were right.* She lunged forward, ready to burn the evil excuse for a human into ash.

Unfortunately, the human was fast. Swinging his bat, he struck her in the side of the jaw. Her fireball went wide, as he raced back to the village with a laugh. Whirling around, Rocket spewed fire at him again. But the crafty human dodged, and instead, one of the village houses went up with a heart-stopping WHOOM!

For a moment, Rocket froze, fearing the damage. She wasn't there to hurt the other humans! What had she done? And then it seemed like time slowed down.

She saw Luco racing back towards the village people, who were staring at the burning building in stunned shock. Off to the side, Blaze stood protectively between Rocket and the children, as the little ones ran screaming back to their parents.

"HELP!" Luco yelled. "SHE'S GONE CRAZY!"

Rocket wanted to pursue. She wanted to explain that he was the threat, not her. So many things were happening all at once. And then, Blaze charged.

The yellow dragon caught Rocket on her blind side. Rocket was hit full force and cartwheeled off her feet.

Rocket tried to take flight, but the yellow dragon drove her down into the ground. She could taste dirt and grass in her mouth as

Blaze pushed her head down and pinned her wings back. She couldn't work an advantage; things were happening too quickly. As Rocket struggled against her yellow counterpart, she saw the humans backing away, looks of terror across their faces.

"MY HOUSE!" Mr. Walker screamed, running to the building Rocket had charbroiled, before turning to a gasping Luco in disbelief. "W-Why?"

Rocket tried to fight back. Tried to push up; tried to speak. This was not how it was supposed to go. But Blaze forced her head back into the ground, trapping her wings and body in a submission hold Drake taught them. She knew better than this, but her mind was spinning. What was happening?

"I-I don't know," Luco said to the assembled people, his voice dripping with feigned fear. "We were just talking…" He pointed his baseball bat at her. "And she suddenly attacked me!"

Gasps rippled through the town. Mothers pulled their children away, and fathers planted themselves before their wives. A few of the villagers looked back at where Luco had led Rocket, as if they knew the truth, but with the smoke drifting across the crowd from the burning structure, they didn't speak up.

"That doesn't make sense," one of the villagers said. "General Drake said they were our saviors."

Luco shook his head, turning back to Rocket. "How could you do this, Rocket?" he bemoaned. "I thought we were friends."

Rocket snarled, fire shooting out of her nostrils in an attempt to singe him. *I thought the same thing, you traitor,* she wanted to scream at him.

Unfortunately, her fire died before it could touch him, and he turned away as Blaze got Rocket in a chokehold, further cutting off her flames.

"Ladies and gentlemen," he said to the villagers. "I do sincerely apologize for this. Rest assured, General Drake will be hearing of this, and she will be properly disciplined."

"You're the one who needs discipline!" Rocket tried to roar. But Blaze's chokehold was tight, and all that sputtered out of Rocket's mouth was a sharp gag. Luco glared at her.

"Save your voice for Drake," he said, hopping onto Blaze. "Let's go Blazy Boo."

"Wait!" the human Luco had been talking to protested. "What about my house?"

"Oh, trust me, Mr. Walker," Luco declared. "When we finish that business, we were discussing, you can get your house back, and more."

That was the last thing Rocket heard before Blaze dragged her out of the village, the jeers and angry words of the humans following after her.

"Blaze," Rocket hissed, struggling in her grip. "You can't…"

"Save it for Drake," Blaze hissed right back, her fire heating up Rocket's neck.

Despite the heat, Rocket felt a chill settle in her gut. *Drake. What was he going to say about this?*

#

Rocket quickly found out; being flung at the foot of Drake's dragon statue throne. As Drake glared down at her with his fiery eyes, Rocket had to resist the urge to curl into a ball and beg his forgiveness.

"General Drake, this dragon has gone rogue!" Luco declared. "She attacked me and set fire to a poor human's house."

"General, please, the King told me that he was bad!" Rocket protested. "He…"

"ENOUGH!" Drake boomed.

Luco and Rocket went silent. While the King had a quieter authority to him, when Drake spoke, everyone listened. The General rose, flexing his powerful arms, entwined with tattoos of dragons.

"Rocket," he said. "Go to the back." He jutted his thumb at the area behind the throne. "I'll be back there shortly to discuss this with you."

"My General…" Rocket tried to interject.

"Now."

Rocket flinched at his tone, and bowed her head, obeying his command.

Luco shook his head as she left. "I'm telling you, General," Luco said. "That one really isn't fit for…"

"Luco," Drake growled, silencing the rider. "Quit the sass, and tell me what happened."

Rocket grimaced and moved faster, not wanting to hear how Luco would build her up as some sort of villain.

Thankfully, she had something to distract her. As she walked into the back of the throne room – where the General slept and ate – she found someone waiting for her.

A woman with a harsh face, scarred from what looked like many battles. Her jet-black was stylized into dreadlocks, and pulled back in a ponytail. The rest of her body was garbed in gray camouflage with dark blue armor pads; fit for someone who needed to move around quickly and quietly. A belt of bolas and hand restrainers adorned her hips.

"Ignis-Drake R065?" the woman asked, standing straight up and saluting. "Agent Valerie Fawkes. I come on behalf of King Connors." She glanced behind Rocket. Both of them could hear the conversation taking place.

"And then for no good reason, just out of the blue… Blaze, demonstrate please?"

The sound of flames emanated.

Rocket growled, while Fawkes had the good sense to grimace.

"I'd ask if you were alright," Fawkes noted. "But considering…"

Rocket sighed. "Your King was right," she growled, rubbing her jaw. "I still can't believe it. The way he talked about what he had done?" Her scales glowed with rage. "Like it was something to be proud of?"

"Take it easy," the agent said firmly, pulling Rocket's head up and lifting a bottle to her lips. "Swallow this."

Obediently, Rocket opened her mouth, and the agent shook some pills into her maw. She reluctantly swallowed, but breathed a sigh of relief as the pain in her jaw from Luco's strike and Blaze's attack faded.

"I could've gotten him," she growled. "But Blaze..." she shook her head. "I've never had to fight her like that before. It was always... friendly sparring. She never..."

"She's loyal," a voice replied, causing Rocket to jump as General Drake joined them. "Just like you are loyal to Buck." He glared at Fawkes. "I don't like this. Your King's being a toxic influence on my dragons."

"All he wants is peace," Fawkes insisted. "Something Luco would rather see wrecked."

Drake grimaced, before looking at Rocket. "Is that true, Rocket? Why did you attack him?"

Rocket looked Drake in the eye, for the first time without fear. "Luco admitted that the King was right," she said. "Then Luco mocked Buck; said that Buck deserved to die because he wasn't strong enough. He taunted me, and I went after him, and then there was some collateral damage…"

Rocket paused, awaiting a reaction. But Drake just listened without emotion.

Fawkes' voice interjected. "I'm guessing this would be the part where the King would say something about the importance of peace."

"Peace is important," Drake replied. "But not weakness. We must not allow our sympathies to blind us to what's true."

"General, please," Rocket insisted. "The King was right about Luco. He's turning us against each other."

Drake pondered, before turning back to Rocket. "I understand that you and the King believe this," he said. "But I don't know what to believe."

Rocket's ears flattened.

"So, I want you to just take some time," Drake continued. "I'm going to find you a new rider, and I don't want you getting involved with Luco, the humans or the wolves until further notice."

Fawkes stepped up to the General. "The King has a recommendation regarding that rider."

Thinking of Shiva, Rocket grimaced. "I don't want her help."

"I know," Fawkes admitted. "But you do need it."

Rocket seethed, but her eyes fell back towards the throne room.

Blaze and Luco were preparing to fly away – the anarchist in deep conversation with another rider. Luco pointed back at Rocket like she was some kind of criminal. And when the other rider looked back… Rocket felt the suspicion in the rider's eyes.

A sense of desperation fell over her. *No one is going to believe me. How can we stop a man who's lies are so convincing?* Her gaze returned to Fawkes and Drake, who's looks were far from encouraging.

"Who is the King recommending?" she asked.

Chapter 2: Myst

Even though Myst created the Pack Link, it never failed to amaze her. As the rain pitter-pattered across the leaf canopy above and splattered through the threads of light that jumped from demi-wolf to demi-wolf, the night-black demi-wolf tensed in anticipation for the electrical shocks that should have followed. The pack link looked so similar to lightning, yet rain was able to fall on it without harming them. Another anomaly of the magic that created them; a magic she barely understood but did her best to use to keep her pack safe.

"Myst," Luke's voice whispered through the link. *"Stay focused."*

Blinking out of her thoughts, Myst redirected her gaze from the pack link threads to the prey ahead. A magnificent male moose, towering over them, six feet at his shoulder. Back and forth the bull tossed his massive antlers; at least five feet across. His small eyes burned with a vicious and paranoid light, and he roared with a fury that chilled Myst's bones. Had she been alone, she might have backed further into the soaked hornbeam and serviceberry shrubs that blanketed the forest floor and left the beast to its own devices. But she was not alone; she had a pack.

Luke, ever the loyal pack-brother, flanked to the moose's right. Shiva, the source of the pack link, stood further back, but her presence was felt in the white energy threads that kept them tied together. And the two newest members of their pack, now adolescents and able to accompany the adults on the hunt; Celine, eagerly crept towards the moose's back, while her brother Kodo held her back with an irritated growl.

"I got him," Celine's voice whispered through the link. *"Just a quick leap onto the back and a run across until I reach the jugular in his neck. I'll be right at his throat. Mama, Papa, you watch?"*

"Stay back, Celine," Luke growled, as the moose stamped his hooves and bellowed, nearly circling right to Celine. *"Wait for our command."*

"We've been chasing this beast for hours," Celine complained. *"I can take him down, you'll see. You'll be so proud!"*

"Celine!" Kodo snapped. *"He said wait!"* He looked to Myst. *"Alpha Myst, we should wait, right?"*

"Indeed, young Kodo," Myst agreed. *"Patience is the greatest of our tools right now."*

"But..." Celine still tried to protest.

"Celine." The stern, yet gentle voice of Shiva echoed through the link. *"Listen to your pack. Glory does not lie in the victory of the one, but the success of the many."*

As she lectured, the moose turned right, squaring off with the two young pups. Myst tensed, yet while Celine was distracted by her mother's voice, her brother was not. Myst felt a surge of concern as Kodo prematurely jumped out of the bushes. Instead of hitting anything vital, Kodo's claws carved deep into the moose's snout, sending it into a frothing rage.

"Kodo!" Shiva barked.

The moose roared and stomped at the moonlight-white form darting away into the brush. Myst rose from the foliage and carved another cut across the moose's flank, drawing its attention away from the young wolf.

The wounds and pursuit were taking a toll, as the moose's head dipped lower. Before it could fully turn to Myst, Luke lunged from the foliage and struck the already battered flanks.

The moose swung its antlered head, eyes glittering, but his swing missed, and his head dipped lower. Myst scored another strike to the back of his legs, and the moose's nose touched the ground. With ears drooped, a mournful groan emanated from deep within his lungs.

As the wolves circled the moose, both sides waited for the next move.

"Can't we get this over with?" Celine pleaded. *"The poor guy's miserable."*

"This is the cruel nature of the wild, Celine," Myst replied. *"He can't go down without a fight, but we can't just let him go and expect to survive ourselves."*

"Myst is right, Celine," Kodo agreed. *"Just look at the guy. His meat will be enough to feed ten packs."*

"Then let's finish him," Celine insisted. *"One good strike. I can take him down, and then he's ours. Please, I can almost feel his pain."*

The demi-wolves exchanged glances with each other, before Luke turned his gaze to Shiva.

"Shiva," Luke whispered. *"Do you think she's ready?"*

A flurry of emotions made the pack link tremble between them. Myst felt Shiva's motherly instinct fight against her grim understanding of the world. A knowledge that if the mother didn't let the daughter grow, she'd leave her beloved child unprepared for the real world.

The world won't be as kind as you can be, Shiva, Myst found herself thinking.

If Shiva heard Myst's thoughts, she didn't let on. Instead, she said. *"Just make it quick, Celine."*

Celine straightened. She came out of the brushes, her golden body tensed. The moose made one last valiant attempt to escape, breaking free of the circle, out of the brush and into the clearing, with Celine in hot pursuit.

Just as Celine sprung for his back, Myst's nose twitched. Another scent was on the wind; a scent Myst wished she never had to smell again, but one she was ready for.

"Celine!" Myst barked, but her voice was drowned out by a sound like thunder. The moose wailed and tumbled backward onto Celine as she scrambled to get out of its way. A small red dot was on his side; a bullet had just punched through his thick hide.

"SISTER!" Kodo barked, jumping to his sister's defense. As he and Luke ran to where the moose had pinned the young wolf, Myst spun to the source of the thunder, her teeth baring up the gums.

She spotted the source of the gunshot; a human. The human was wrapped in camouflage fatigues, but they did nothing to conceal him from Myst.

This was what she was for. This was her place; on the front lines, against those that would see her kind caged or dead. With a mighty lunge, the night-black demi-wolf knocked the hunter's next shot off course. She pinned the human under his rifle, and pressed the weapon down against the surprised, struggling human's neck.

"Filthy human," Myst's thoughts snarled, as she tried to crush his neck. *"Pretentious, self-serving, high and mighty..."*

"MYST!" Shiva boomed, her voice carrying an anger that reminded Myst of bad memories. *Of when humans would boom at her, usually followed by fists and boots.*

But Myst would not be cowed. Not again. Not by...

She paused. It wasn't a human ordering her to stop; it was one of her own. One of her beloved pack. Taking a deep breath, Myst forced herself to calm.

"It's a human, Shiva," Myst insisted, as the hunter gagged and kicked under her cruel vice. *"It shot at your daughter!"*

"Let me use the link on him!" Shiva insisted. *"Before you do anything, let's figure out why he's here."*

"You would let him live after he attacked her?!" Myst snarled, her anger bubbling closer to the surface.

"I said, let me use the link on him," Shiva's bark was out loud and her tone dissuaded protest from even the former Alpha.

Then Luke's voice sounded. "Myst."

Myst looked to her pack mate, careful not to let the hunter go. Luke lifted up Celine; though the golden demi-wolf looked ruffled, she was otherwise unharmed.

"She's fine," Luke insisted, going back to speaking through the Pack Link. *"Now see what he's really here for. We should at least know if he's got friends."*

"His friends won't cause trouble if we use him for an example," Kodo pointed out.

"Kodo, that's enough!" both Luke and Shiva growled at him.

Myst's ears flattened at the wolves shutting down her one ally and growled in dissatisfaction.

"Please…" the hunter was whimpering. "Please… I was… I didn't know… please…"

Myst glared down at him with utter contempt. Humans; always so smug and superior when they thought they had the upper hand. But the minute she got even the smallest advantage over them, they were reduced to pathetic, crying babies; either screaming that the rules weren't fair, or begging for mercy.

It sickened her; all she wanted was to press down even harder. To watch the life fade from his eyes and his struggles slowly spasm to nothing.

But Shiva wouldn't allow that. No, the soft-hearted wolf still somehow held pity for these things. And even now, Myst could feel Shiva's presence in the link, ready to yank Myst away if she tried to hurt the human. With a growl of discontent, Myst relaxed her grip, taking the human's face in her claws so he couldn't get away, and letting the pack link tendrils spiral around his head. In seconds, the wolves' heads were filled with memories:

The Hunter's name was John Walker. He made a living off the creatures of the forest. Not just to feed himself, however.

Myst saw a kindly looking wife and three beautiful children. All looking up at the hunter with hope; assurance that he'd bring back something for them.

He wanted to do more for them. He wanted to give them a better life. And so… when a man with a distinctive scar across his mouth came to him…

Myst's claws tightened; she knew that scar. She had seen it in her nightmares, rippling with his laughter as he tormented her.

"Luco," Myst growled. Her claws tensed, digging into the hunter's skull and eliciting a groan of pain.

"Give me a minute," Shiva insisted, as the visions continued.

They saw a red dragon, fire spurting from her maw and setting a house alight. Walker's house.

Shiva paused. "Rocket…?" she muttered.

But the vision continued. *With his house gone, Walker was desperate. And Luco's deal was so simple. "Just go into the woods," Luco proposed. "Attack them. I will be there; I will protect you. Do that, and you'll get your house back and more."*

But as Myst snapped out of the vision and looked around, she saw Luke was already ahead of her, scanning the woods.

The yellow demi-wolf shook his head. *"No sign of anyone else,"* he reported. *"The foolish human's alone."* He glanced down at Walker in pity. "What happened to your friend?"

Walker blinked. "W-What friend?"

"The guy with the scar," Luke said. "The one who sent you here."

Walker paled. "How did…"

Myst growled, killing the man's curiosity.

"I was just doing a job," the man said quickly. "I didn't know who he was… please!"

"He was working for 'Him,' Shiva," Myst insisted.

"He said he didn't know."

"Look harder. Tell me you really believe that."

"I'm looking, and I know what I saw."

"And you're still going to let him go?" Kodo demanded.

"Kodo, don't start," Shiva ordered. *"I know what I'm doing."*

Myst growled. *"Should I give him the moose while you're at it?"*

"No. Let him find prey elsewhere."

Myst sighed; at least Shiva wasn't a complete idiot. She shifted as she felt Shiva's next words go past her and into the hunter's head. *"Now you listen to me, John Walker. That man with the scar sent you here to die. Don't you ever listen to him again – no matter what the offer is. Because the next time you come across our territory, I won't stop her."*

John Walker felt Myst's presence looming over him and nodded. "O-Of course," he stammered. "I'll leave you be. I promise."

Liar, Myst thought with a growl. But she felt Shiva's presence again.

Release him, Shiva ordered. *Like I said, you can kill him if he comes back.*

Myst smirked, remembering when a human ignored Shiva's mercy. The beautiful silence in the link as Shiva wordlessly allowed Myst to cleanse this world of at least one more human.

Yes, Myst decided, this human would come back. She'd get rid of him then. Shiva would see; she'd understand.

With her thoughts comforting her, Myst relinquished her grip on the hunter. The pack link tendrils faded away, and the hunter scrambled up. Raising his hands, he ran as fast as his legs could carry him, the trees swallowing him up as he desperately fled for his family.

Myst let another grumble slip out of her snout, before Kodo gently nuzzled at her side. Myst turned to him, eyes soft, and patted his shoulder, before following him back to Luke and Celine. She nosed Celine gently, checking her for injuries.

"Are you okay, Celine?" she asked.

Celine wagged her tail at the elder wolf. "Just great," she said.

Kodo sighed. "You're too reckless for your own good," he noted. "I swear, sometimes it feels like you like scaring the crap out of me."

Celine gave her brother a grin. "Your reactions are pretty priceless."

Kodo huffed, while Myst gave the forest another look over; even though the hunter was gone, his stink still permeated the woods.

"Either way, good work," Myst said. "You guys get the moose back to the others. I'm going to go make sure that hunter actually left."

Kodo immediately perked up. "I'll go with you," he said.

Instantly, Myst felt a twinge at the back of her skull, like Shiva was glaring at her. *"Don't try anything with my son,"* she warned.

"Shiva, come on," Myst said, grinning as Kodo bounced up to her side. "I'm not just the Killer of Men; I'm the Hero of Wolves, remember?"

"He'll be fine, Shiva," Luke assured her. "Myst looked after me and the others like we were her children. Kodo's going to be perfectly safe."

Despite his words, Myst could still feel Shiva's powers tightening around her like the worst kind of leash.

"You don't stray from the edge of our territory," Shiva growled. *"And if there's trouble…"*

"He'll be safe," Myst insisted.

"And getting out of work," Celine grumbled as she struggled with the moose. "Seriously… Didn't wolves normally just eat these guys on the spot? Why can't Mom just come back and we can eat here?"

"It's not just for us," Luke reminded her, easily hefting the moose onto his back. "It's for the other mothers and pups. Not every pup is ready for hunting like you."

"They should be," Kodo muttered.

Celine grimaced. "They were only born a few weeks ago."

"And how old were you before you started trying to sneak out?" Kodo asked with a grin.

"I had the pack link!" Celine insisted.

"So, do they."

"You know what I mean," Celine barked, as her own pack link spiraled to life. Seizing Kodo by the neck, he tripped over his paws, and hit the ground.

"Hey!" Kodo barked, grabbing the tendrils and binding them with threads of his own.

The two started struggling in a tug of war, before Myst got between them.

"Children-children, please!" Myst barked. "We have work to do!"

Celine wriggled and tried to pull regardless. But her young body didn't have as much strength as Myst. And with a grin, Myst stamped on her tendril, easily pulling the wolf to the ground.

"No fair!" she bemoaned, as Kodo grinned smugly at her.

"Now," Myst said, turning to Kodo. "Can we get on with this?"

His smile fading, Kodo nodded, following Myst as she traced the human's scent. As the human's stench trailed past their borders and beyond, Myst sat, sighing in disappointment. Kodo scratched the ground before sitting next to her, grimacing in thought.

"You okay, Kodo?" Myst asked.

"Why do you and Mom hate each other?" Kodo asked. His ears flattened when Myst raised an eyebrow at him. "I-I mean, not that it's my business, but…"

"It's okay," Myst assured him, looking back at the horizon. "And don't worry; I don't hate your mom. Things are just… complicated between us."

Kodo hummed. "So… you're not going to hurt each other?"

Myst looked right at him. "Never," she promised. "No matter how soft Shiva is for the humans… she is my pack-sister. I consider her family." She smiled softly. "And if there's one thing we agree on, it's that family is all that matters."

Kodo's tail wagged, and the two looked back. Though they couldn't see the demi-wolf community from where they were, Myst could still envision it: a sprawling village with dens carved into trees and caves. The pack link hung over the settlement like human powerlines, linking to wolves as they cooked meals, trained pups, or just watched them play.

At the forefront of it all, sitting at the entrance to a den carved into the roots of a mighty and ancient evergreen tree, Shiva herself sat, her fur glowing like a goddess.

Myst sighed. Despite all the pain and anger that still bubbled and burned in her gut, she knew that Shiva made the right call in giving them a home; a sanctuary. A place where Myst and all the other wolves could stop, catch their breaths, and be reminded of why they fought so hard to get away from the cruel humans. She patted Kodo's head.

"Don't worry about your parents," she assured him. "No matter what comes our way, we'll figure it out together."

Kodo grinned up at her... but his grin faded.

Myst tilted her head, before she realized he wasn't looking at her. Following his gaze, her eyes widened as she spotted a strange red scaled bird.

No, not a bird, Myst realized, as she lifted her head to howl for Shiva, *a dragon.*

Rocket.

They saw her; Rocket was sure of it. Having entered White Fang Wood, she was unable to shake the feeling that the eyes of every wolf were upon her. Of course, a big red dragon flying over the top of a forest was not the most discreet way to approach, but Connors insisted on her being visible; all the better to convey her intentions were pure.

She felt like the wind pressed against her scales was whispering, 'Go back.' The chill of the sky battled her natural body warmth. She felt her courage slipping.

This was a stupid idea! She thought. *How can I trust the demi-wolves? I've been fighting them my whole life. They're supposed to be my mortal enemies!*

She recalled Drake's first words to her: *"No one else can stop them. But you, Rocket, you will be the one to put an end to their reign of terror."*

And yet, at the same time, they… weren't really doing anything bad anymore. Granted, they were killing deer and moose, but humans did the same thing. Heck, that one human was responsible for the big moose going down, and *Myst herself* had let him go.

Maybe I was wrong to judge Shiva so harshly, Rocket thought. *She certainly seems to have turned the wolves around. Maybe this isn't such a bad idea after all.*

Then a howl sounded.

Rocket almost laughed as a pack link tendril flashed like a lightning bolt and cinched around the girth of her neck. *Or-I-was-right-all-along-and-they're-about-to-try-and-kill-me!* Rocket squelched a roar as she was drawn into a forest clearing.

She remembered – and not happily – Shiva's pack link getting into her mind, despite her best efforts to resist.

She flipped, landing like a cat with fire burning in her talons. But when she looked around, it didn't look like the same forest clearing. A pale ivory cast a glow and shade on everything. It was as if a dusting of snow dropped with Rocket and blanketed the forest floor. She could still see dark trunks rising up above her, and the sky was tinted in a slight blue-gray hue. But everything else was blinding white. Strangely, it wasn't cold, though. Not that Rocket would've cared – her fire would keep her warm regardless – but for a place that looked like it was covered in snow, the frost didn't seem all that icy. A low hum sang in the background, but Rocket couldn't hear other noises; no birds or squirrels or even the wind. Just that low, song-like hum.

Rocket didn't have much time to ponder her odd surroundings. She looked around, perusing the frosty clearing, before three familiar wolves appeared before her. The snow-white visage of Shiva, the night-black frame of Myst, and a sunset-yellow demi-wolf that Rocket vaguely recalled as having a nasty habit of jumping on her back and biting her.

For a moment, they regarded her like hunters. Rocket spread her wings, ready for Shiva and Myst to start flanking her. Her tail whipped behind her, just in case they had more wolves hoping to jump on her. But the wolves didn't move to attack nor to retreat. They seemed to be waiting for her to make the first move.

Rocket felt her neck and found the pack link wound around her throat. It had formed some sort of collar, which she tried to pull on.

"What is this?!" Rocket demanded. "What did you do to me?"

"Relax, Rocket." Shiva's voice seemed to sound all around her. "This is a mental bridge. The pack link was first and foremost about connecting minds. I've simply used the time I've had out here to refine it."

Rocket huffed. "Saying 'hello' would be a lot simpler."

The yellow one – Luke, Rocket believed he was called – hummed. "That's true," he realized before waving at her. "Hello."

She narrowed her eyes. "Was that sarcasm?"

"Depends," Myst replied. "What are you doing flying above our territory?"

Shiva scoffed. "Myst, please. Why ask when we can just find out?" She made a clenching motion with her claw.

Rocket blinked as the pack link turned red. A voice whispered in her head. *Why are you here?* And as she thought of Luco, her anger faded to shock as a small square image appeared between the dragon and the wolves.

Rocket gaped. *She was looking at herself. Luco grinning up at her.*

"Of course, you don't realize it at first," he said. "Like Myst. You won't believe how long she clung to her fleeting hope. The

amount of time it took me to beat out any sympathy she held for humans?" He whistled and chuckled. *"I couldn't lift my arms for a week."*

Myst's fur bristled, and her teeth bared at his words.

"But it was worth it," Luco whispered out of the memory, *spreading his arms out to the countryside like he wanted to hold it for himself. "She did better than I could have hoped for. And when Drake sent you – his guardians, his honest souls?"* He chuckled. *"The battles were epic!"*

"The battles were sick!" Rocket's past version hissed. *"People died! My Rider died!"*

Luco turned back to her, his eyes glittering with cruelty. "Then I guess he wasn't worth his salt as a fighter."

Rocket's scales glowed with rage as the memory continued; showing her chasing Luco. She winced when Blaze caught her off guard and pinned her down. And when the crowd gathered...

"How could you do this, Rocket?" Luco whimpered with *feigned distress. "I thought we were friends."*

The image faded back into white as Rocket shut her eyes. *"I really hoped that you weren't right about Luco,"* she thought. *"But..."*

"But the truth is hard to hide," Myst said.

Rocket looked up in shock, but for once, the black wolf didn't look smug.

Myst stepped forward. "Are you here about Luco?"

Rocket straightened, unsure whether to be pleased or put off. "The... King wants your help tracking him down."

Shiva looked around. "Then where is he? Why can't he ask us himself?"

Rocket merely looked at Myst. Myst rolled her eyes, while Shiva chuckled.

"Right."

"Believe me, I didn't like it either," Rocket said, as her memories reappeared: *The King standing before her.*

"Rocket," he had said. "I want you to take a wolf as your new rider."

All three wolves bristled in shock. "You want WHAT?!" Myst's voice shouted.

"After everything we were put through?" Luke demanded, memories appearing from both of them: *dragons attacking them. Raining down fire from above.*

"Didn't I just say I didn't like it either?!" Rocket argued back, her own memories rushing forward to combat the wolves: *her yelling 'no' at the King, wolves swarming her, bringing down her fellow dragons and humans...*

"ENOUGH!" Shiva barked, dispelling the images. "This isn't about politics; this is about taking down Luco. Setting aside our differences and focusing on the real threat."

Myst's teeth bared and she turned back to Shiva with bristling fur.

"And what would you have us do?" Myst demanded. "Play along with that blind General and that conniving King?"

"Watch yourself," Rocket growled, but Myst didn't even glance her way, her comments directed at Shiva.

"Subject Luco to some court where he can sweet-talk the crowd or make some sort of deal with the judge?"

"And what if you kill the wrong person… again," Shiva growled back. Briefly, Shiva's memory of an older human flashed between them, before Luke stepped in.

"Okay, enough of that," he said, looking up to Rocket. "So, you're going after Luco, you need help, and Connors wants our help. Correct?"

Rocket winced, her memories showing Luco striking her with the bat. "Unfortunately, yes. I can't take Luco on alone… and I don't want to risk another human life."

Shiva's ears drooped, and she looked away from Rocket. Myst, however, narrowed her eyes.

"But you're fine risking our lives?" she noted.

Rocket's eyes narrowed. The golden-eyed demi-wolf matched her glare.

"Tell me something, dragon," Myst said darkly. "When you came out of your egg, and were told my demi-wolves and I were villains… did that help blind you from the fact that you were made to end lives?"

Rocket snarled. "I was made to protect lives!"

"Human lives," Myst scoffed. "Let's take a dive back into those memories of yours."

Rocket felt a sensation like Myst's claws tapping along her skull. She pulled back, but the memories returned despite her resistance.

This time, it showed *Rocket and her rider Buck, side by side as her fire lit up a forest.* Rocket remembered the stench of not just burning wood, but cooking meat. Cries echoed in her ears. The taste of ash danced on her tongue. In the image, *a demi-wolf shot out of the brush, shrieking. His fur was aflame, turning him into a canine torch. And as the memory showed Rocket focusing on him, a smile crossed her snout, tongues of fire licked at her teeth, and...*

Rocket looked away, but looking away only allowed her to see the expressions of disgust on Luke and even Shiva's faces. It sent a shiver down her spine; at the time, she felt so proud of herself. She was protecting people. She was making Buck and Drake proud. But now, under the gaze of those she had hurt...

"It felt good, didn't it?" Myst noted. "Satisfying, to see the downfall of those you considered 'villain.' But take another look."

A ball of light formed in Myst's claws, and she threw it at Rocket's feet. The ball changed into another memory. *This time, a past version of Myst had a human pressed against the bars of a cage. Inside the cage, an unaltered dog was backed up against the opposite wall, quivering in fear. Lines of red dripped down his body, and when the dog gazed at the human, there was anger hidden among the terror.*

The anger burned brighter in the memory of Myst's eyes, as she forced the man's head harder into the bars. The man's terrified screams filled Rocket's ears. But she saw the evidence of what else he had done. Bloodied clubs; ominous wriggling sacks. This man did not just hurt the dog in the cage, but countless others. A chill shot through Rocket's guts as, *in the image, Myst's teeth bared, and she finished it.*

Rocket swallowed. Why did seeing that human die feel so… right? Why did she feel… like he deserved it? Myst smiled at the dragon's conflict.

"You see?" she asked. "I saw that human the same way you saw us. I felt the same way you did when I rescued that dog from his filthy hands." She lifted her claws. "Which one of us is the righteous defender, Rocket?"

Rocket bristled, wanting to argue, before Shiva stepped in.

"That's enough, Myst," Shiva barked. "Rocket may have prioritized humans, but you prioritized demi-wolves. You're not any better or any worse than she was."

Myst snarled at Shiva, but Luke once again stood in her way.

"All excellent points to think about," he said neutrally. "But they won't matter if Luco is allowed to turn us against each other again." He turned to Rocket. "Dragon; can you promise that whoever we send with you will be returned in one piece?"

"And who are you going to send?" Myst asked, her glare not leaving Shiva. "Certainly, not Shiva or one of her pups."

Shiva's fur spiked, and even Luke had to resist baring his teeth. Rocket, however, blinked in shock.

"Pups?" she asked, staring at Shiva. "You have pups already?"

"Very young ones," Shiva's eyes narrowed. "Who are 'not' ready for something like this." She breathed, calming herself, and forced her gaze away from Myst and to Rocket. "And I'm the source of the pack link, which is running most of our community. I can't leave."

"If you want the job done right, you'll send me," Myst said.

Rocket bristled. "I don't trust you."

Myst turned away with a snort, while Rocket looked hopefully to Luke. The male was scratching his chin, pondering, before he noticed Rocket's gaze.

"Oh-ho, not me," he laughed, jutting a claw at the two females. "Without me, these two would rip each other to shreds."

Myst and Shiva huffed and turned up their noses, but didn't refute him. Rocket sat back with a grumble.

"I need someone who's capable of taking on Luco and Blaze," Rocket insisted, remembering the yellow dragon. "Since Blaze is going to be defending Luco… it's going to take a lot to bring those two down."

For a moment, the wolves were silent. Myst and Shiva stood with their backs to each other, while Luke kept himself between them. After a conflicted glance at Shiva, Myst sighed.

"I have unfinished business with Luco," Myst said. "And I don't want to risk him getting his hands on another one of my pack."

Shiva glowered. "And how can we trust that you'll do things Rocket's way?" she asked.

Rocket stiffened. "I hate to admit it, but Shiva's right. I want Luco to face proper justice; I want him to stand before Connors, confess his crimes, and go down as the criminal he is."

Myst groaned. "You've made this too complicated! If we just…"

Shiva barked, silencing Myst's protests. "If we're going to let you go with Rocket – which I'm not comfortable with – then you need to promise us that you will do things Rocket's way."

Luke interjected. "And the dragon has to promise that Myst will come back in one piece."

Rocket tilted her head at the look of conflict on Myst's face. The dragon had always dismissed the night-black demi-wolf as a murderer; someone that was only satisfied when she was either taking human lives or sending demi-wolves out for her insane quest. Yet now, Myst looked almost… afraid. Like the idea of sending another demi-wolf out was too great a sacrifice.

Myst lowered her head, taking a long, slow breath. For a moment, she was silent. However, right as Shiva turned away, Myst spoke.

"Fine."

All eyes fell on the wolf as she regarded Rocket.

"If you promise not to betray me," Myst said. "I vow to work with you to take down Luco."

Rocket cocked an eyebrow. "Serious?" she asked.

Myst pointed at her. "If you give me your word that you've got my back."

Rocket grimaced, before she noticed Luke watching her expectantly. Rocket was silent at first, but after a long pause…

"I'll still be connected to her with the pack link," Shiva said. "If Myst does try to go rogue or hurt anyone, I'll stop her."

Rocket's frown deepened; she didn't like any of this. She hated the fact that she was hunting a human; she despised that she had to ask the wolves for help. And she abhorred how eager Myst looked to begin the hunt.

But the thought of Luco's cackle – his utter dismissal of Buck's death – steeled Rocket's nerves.

"Alright then," the dragon said. "I'm in."

Myst, Shiva and Luke all nodded. And with a motion from Shiva's claw, the white void faded away.

#

Rocket's eyes opened. She was lying on a soft brown forest floor. The trees rose above her, forming a bright green leaf canopy that sparkled with the orange rays of a setting sun. Rocket lifted herself to a sitting position, shivering as dirt ran down her scales, before someone cleared her throat.

Rocket blinked the sleep from her eyes. Myst was holding out a claw for her, the star-like spots on her fur glittering in the setting sun.

"On your feet," Myst growled. "We have a terrorist to catch."

Chapter 4: Allies

Three minutes earlier…

If Myst had not created the pack link, she was sure things would have gone far worse. Her howl would have likely been heard by the dragon just as it had by her fellow demi-wolves. And by the time they were able to organize an attack, Rocket would have charbroiled the forest.

Despite Shiva's aggravating sympathy for humans, her reflexes were fast as a cobra's strike. And Myst was able to watch in satisfaction as a pack link tendril shot up from Shiva and wound around the dragon's neck. Instantly, the reptile went limp, and plummeted into the forest.

Kodo stood nearby. Myst put a claw on his shoulder. "Go back to the others," Myst ordered. "Stay close to your mom."

"Can't I help?" he asked.

"Yes. By protecting your sister and the younglings."

Where Celine might have groaned at such a task, Kodo's eyes narrowed with determination. "You can count on me, Alpha," he promised, before he turned and leaped into the foliage.

Grinning at Kodo's loyalty, Myst sprinted to where the dragon landed. She soon found Rocket, curled up on the ground. The dragon's eyes were shut, and small puffs of smoke rose from her snout like snores. A collar of light was bound around her neck, with smaller, spark-like tendrils digging into her scales.

Grabbing the link, Myst sunk into the bridge between minds.

#

As the telepathic conference concluded, Shiva held Myst back.

"You listen to her," Shiva warned. "And don't even think about going after any humans other than Luco."

Myst looked away with a glower, before she felt Luke touch her mind.

"You can do this, Myst," he said. "Once Luco's taken care of, I'm sure we'll all rest a lot easier."

Myst chuckled. "In a way, this has been a long time coming," she said, glancing at Shiva. "All those humans I killed; they were… in my way to finding Luco. When we get him… maybe I'll find some peace."

Shiva's glare didn't falter. "There's a lot riding on this," she said. "For all of us. Don't let us down." She motioned with her claw, and Myst's consciousness left the mental bridge.

And in good time; right as Myst's mind returned to her body, the pack link collar faded from Rocket's neck, and the dragon's electric green eyes fluttered open. Myst cleared her throat, drawing the dragon's gaze, and held out a claw.

"On your feet," Myst said. "We have a terrorist to catch."

Rocket huffed and rose up. "That we do." She glared down at the demi-wolf. "But just so we're clear… we're 'catching' the man. Not killing him."

Myst glared. "And we're going to work together to do that. That means that if I get in trouble, I should be able to count on you." Her eyes narrowed. "Are you going to have my back if that happens?"

Rocket sneered. "Depends. I've got no interest in repeating my last encounter with Blaze and Luco. Will you have 'my' back against them?"

Myst struggled with an answer. Part of her thought this was a stupid idea; having to kowtow to this dragon, this puppet of the humans.

And yet, what was the alternative? Shiva would never let Myst go beyond their territory on her own. This was the first chance Myst had in a long while to hunt for a human.

No, she reminded herself. *Not just any human. 'The' human; the one responsible for my suffering, and the suffering of so many others.*

Myst looked Rocket in the eye. "If it comes down to it," she promised. "I'll keep you safe."

Rocket huffed. "We'll see."

Myst rolled her eyes, and headed towards the boundary of White Fang Wood.

Rocket bristled as the wolf passed by her. "And where are you going?"

Myst looked back. "Are we hunting this scum bag, or what?"

Rocket flared her wings. "It'd be faster to fly."

Myst laughed. "I'm not going anywhere near those flames. I agreed to help you catch Luco, not to get burned."

"Humans fly," Rocket chided. "Are you saying you're not as brave as a human?"

Myst growled, her pride provoked, but the dragon was right. She stepped closer. "You better not drop me."

Rocket put a talon over her heart. "I swear by Teeth-For-Days, anyone who rides me will not fear death by falling."

Myst tilted her head. "Is that some kind of oath?"

Rocket stooped and lowered her wings. "It's a promise."

Myst's ears flattened, but without any other way to protest, she gingerly climbed onto the back of the dragon. Rocket's back was smooth and muscular, with large spines running up her neck. Along her chest and under her wings were small dimples that made for perfect footholds. Myst was easily able to grasp the spines along Rocket's neck, and her paws settled almost naturally into the dimples along Rocket's ribs.

"Hang on," Rocket said, as her entire body warmed like Myst was sitting next to a fire. Myst looked down and spotted Rocket's feet beginning to glow.

"Hey-hey, don't set the forest on fire!" Myst warned.

"Relax," Rocket said. "I've done this a million times." She kicked off from the ground, a brief burst of flames propelling her forward. But as Myst watched, the flames followed after Rocket, creating a vortex that, together with her powerful wings, drove Rocket up into the sky.

Images of her time captured – being hauled through the sky – came back to Myst, and she gripped Rocket's spines tighter. Struggling against the latent fear, Myst focused on trusting the dragon. She found herself wondering what it must be like for Rocket – having lost Buck, and now having to carry Myst – once her enemy.

She thought back to Rocket's vow… and grimaced. "What even is that?"

"Huh?"

"Teeth-For-Days," Myst said. "Every time something goes wrong for you dragons, you always spout that, 'Teeth-For-Days' Fangs.' 'I swear by Teeth-For-Days.' Is Teeth-For-Days important or something?"

Rocket snorted. "Why do you care?"

"If we're going to work together," Myst said. "We should at least be able to hold a conversation."

"We're not friends." Rocket focused on flying. "We'll never be friends after everything you did."

Myst's fur bristled, but she forced herself to stay calm.

"No," she admitted. "We won't be friends. But pack mates don't have to be friends in order to survive."

Rocket was silent at first. Myst bent her head and tried to think of something else aside from the height. But after a minute of silence...

"Teeth-For-Days is an Old One," Rocket said. "He's... I dunno, I guess the humans would call him a God or something." She shrugged. "To me, General Drake will always be God. He's the one that made us." She looked down. "Him and Luco..."

Myst bit her tongue to keep from retorting.

"But a couple of dragons got curious," Rocket continued. "They started reading different stories about dragons. And so... General Drake gave us the story of Teeth-For-Days. And enough of the dragons decided that Teeth-For-Days was a good enough role model that we should look up to him."

Myst chuckled. "So you worship him or pray to him or something?" A new thought made Myst's ears perk. "Is he a dragon too?"

"Of course," Rocket said. "As for praying to him... no, not really."

"Then what's he for?"

Rocket grinned. "He reminds us of why we need Riders."

Myst's ears twitched. She leaned forward to hear better against the wind.

"The story goes that once, dragons didn't have riders," Rocket said. "They claimed they didn't need them. Humans were weak and useless. And the most powerful dragon, Teeth-For-Days, was no exception. But in an epic battle, he was blinded in both eyes, and crashed down to Earth. Without his eyes, it looked like his life was over. But instead, he came across a human – Reacher. Reacher was crippled, but he was wise. Teeth-For-Days found safety with Reacher. And through their bond, they were both able to regain what they had lost: Teeth-For-Days became Reacher's legs, while Reacher became Teeth-For-Days' eyes. And together, the two proved to be more powerful than any other human or dragon alone." Rocket smiled softly. "And ever since, no dragon feels complete without their rider."

Myst pondered her story. "So... does that make me your rider now?"

Rocket was silent at first. "We'll see."

Silence reigned again for a moment, as the wind sang in their ears. Myst found herself thinking about belief, and her thoughts turned to her pack.

"You know," Myst said. "Several of the wolves started seeing Shiva and me as goddesses. I... guess it made sense. I evolved them, Shiva gave them a sanctuary..." Her head lowered. "But I don't like it."

Rocket paused, her ears perking. She turned back. "You don't like being put on a pedestal?" She scoffed. "Now I know you're messing with me."

"I may have evolved them from the dogs they were, but I did it so that they could have control of their own lives. I didn't free them from..." she held back a rant that she felt bubbling up and tried to soften her voice. "I didn't give them freedom; I fought for it."

Rocket hummed. "Sure didn't stop them from doing what you said."

"They had a choice," Myst insisted. "They made it. And in case you didn't notice, not all of them chose to mindlessly agree with me. Look at Shiva."

"Shiva only chose to leave you because she had the Pack Link," Rocket replied. "It's not a very good comparison when no one else had what she had, or what she could offer to others."

Myst wanted to retort, but a nagging sensation in the back of her mind stopped her.

Was it true that she had just become the demi-wolves' master? Did she really deserve the title of Goddess? All she wanted was for them to live a life free from slavery and torment. She had always assumed that their choice to fight was entirely their own.

But was that wrong? Had she unintentionally used her position to scare the demi-wolves into doing what she wanted? Fighting in a war that they didn't actually want?

Her heart sunk as she thought of when Shiva first suggested leaving. How several demi-wolves had gone to Shiva's side. And how plenty others almost tried but cowered and returned to Myst's side when the growling and teeth-baring started.

"I…" Myst mumbled.

But her pondering was cut off when Rocket tucked her wings and dove, and Myst saw a group of humans waiting for them in an open field below.

The dragon did a low turn over the open space, where Myst could see General Drake alongside the hooded visage of King Connors. Another human stood off to the side – a disgruntled looking young woman with jet black hair stylized in a dreadlocked ponytail – but Myst didn't have time to worry about bodyguards.

Rocket landed next to the men, and Myst dismounted. Drake eyes flared at the sight of her.

"Well, there must be a blizzard in Tartarus," Drake said. "A wolf riding a dragon."

"General," Connors chided. "That's enough."

But Drake turned back to him. "Sir, I did not agree to this. A demi-wolf was one thing, but Myst herself?" He pointed at her. "She can't be trusted."

Myst crossed her arms. "Speaking of trust, you and I still have unfinished business, General. You can trust that."

Rocket stepped forward. "Myst, remember your promise."

Connors raised an eyebrow, but his only comment was, "So you're the one Shiva is sending to help us?"

Myst and Drake glared each other down, before Myst took a breath. "If it means Luco goes down," the demi-wolf growled. "I can't say no to stopping him."

"You're only stopping him the way we want it," Drake said darkly. "No fatalities; no unnecessary assaults, and no endangering my dragon or other riders' lives."

Rocket hesitated. "What about Blaze?"

Drake didn't hesitate. "Make every effort you can to bring her back alive. No matter what she's done, she's still one of us."

Myst tried to speak, but her fur suddenly glowed, and Shiva's voice came out from her mouth.

"Don't worry, General," Shiva said. *"My pack link will ensure that Myst stays under control, and that she doesn't do anything that could damage our alliance."*

Drake and the bodyguard stepped back, watching Myst with trepidation. Connors, however, seemed to take the twist in stride.

"Relax, Fawkes," he said to the bodyguard, before turning back to Myst. "And thank you for your aid, Alpha Shiva. You are doing a great service for all of us: human, dragon and demi-wolf."

"Alpha?" Myst seethed, but Connors turned to Drake, and both Drake and Rocket glared at Myst as if daring her to strike.

"General Drake," Connors said, apparently oblivious to Myst's anger, "You have the things from Luco's room?"

Drake frowned but pulled out a bright yellow, short sleeved tropical shirt with a colorful pattern of trees and skulls.

"Luco was more than willing to come to me when Rocket was causing trouble," Drake explained, tossing the shirt toward Myst, and managing to land it right on her snout. "But he's refusing to see the King. The King sent a summons and asked me to make him go, but every time, Luco has either lied and said he's already gone, or found some excuse to weasel out of it."

Connors handed Rocket a sigil; a chain with a flat piece of metal with a hooded eye inscribed on it. "If you run into your fellow dragons," he said, draping it around her neck. "Show them this; it will let them know that you're on official business for me."

"And you will need that." Drake glanced at Connors before returning his gaze to Rocket. "I still really don't like this, Rocket; Luco was one of my best. The man who helped me make the dragons in the first place."

"I understand, my General," Rocket said, "I trusted him once too."

"That's your problem," the bodyguard Fawkes muttered. "Trust. Every time you trust someone, you're just giving them the opportunity to…"

"Agent Fawkes," Connors chastised.

Fawkes went silent, while Drake continued to stare at Myst with suspicion. He turned to Rocket.

"Make sure that this…" He glanced back at Myst's narrowed eyes, "… 'demi-wolf' does her job properly, and that you bring Luco and Blaze in alive."

Rocket nodded. "Blaze's my kin, General," she assured him. "I won't fail again."

"See that you don't," King Connors said. "Especially with regard to Myst's safety." He gave a slight smile to Myst before turning away. "We don't need her or her followers resuming their campaign against us because you were careless with her life."

Rocket snorted, but quickly added a, "Yes, sir."

"Very good," Connors said, turning to walk away. "Despite my bodyguard's beliefs, you have my trust, Myst. I have absolute confidence that you'll handle this. Good luck."

Drake huffed, before walking after Connors. Fawkes followed, glaring at Myst one last time. However, Myst's eyes narrowed as she saw Fawkes come up alongside Connors. With the hearing of a demi-wolf, she just barely managed to pick up Connors speaking to Fawkes.

"Follow them in secret," Connors whispered. "Help them if needed. I won't allow Myst to kill any more humans, but don't risk your life."

"Yes, sir," Fawkes said.

Myst scoffed. *"Humans."* She thought, before lifting Luco's shirt, and breathing in its scent.

"Well?" Rocket asked.

Myst paused, lowering the shirt, and letting the scent merge with the worldly aromas around them. At first, it was difficult to detect among the smell of grasses, trees and shrubs, and the wind carrying odors from every corner of the world. But Myst had followed Luco's stink for years, and after a moment of concentration, the night-black demi-wolf's snout turned like a compass, pointing to the east. She grinned at Rocket.

"Let the hunt begin."

Chapter 5: Luco

As the duo flew over the mountains, tracking Luco, Rocket pondered the furry creature on her back.

Despite being a ferocious fighter, Myst didn't have wings, her fur was a poor excuse for armor, and she was so small. In comparison to Rocket, anyway. It was difficult to see how she could be useful in the coming conflict. Yet, despite all of Rocket's added strengths, she still failed to bring down Luco. To the point that Drake and Connors seemed to think working with Myst was the best plan.

Time would tell, of course, as Luco's scent brought them into the mountains. Despite Rocket's doubts, she had to admit that Myst's tracking abilities were impressive. The way she followed invisible scents for miles and miles seemed magical. But what was magical was the faint glow of the pack link across Myst's fur. The pack link was what gave Myst and the demi-wolves the edge. If it wasn't for the pack link, the dragons could've ended the war a long time ago.

As Rocket considered her fellow dragons, she suddenly spotted one soaring among the clouds. She heard Myst chuckle.

"It seems dear Shiva is confused," she noted.

Rocket glanced back at her. "How do you know?"

Myst indicated the glow in her fur. "Pack Link. Shiva's watching right now. And she doesn't know about all of the dragons that Drake has at his disposal."

Despite herself, Rocket couldn't help but grin. "Then tell her it's a good thing she chose peace. Because fire dragons were the least of her concerns."

Indeed, the dragon above them was far different from the few dragons the white wolf had likely encountered. He was much more like the birds he flew with; a sharp beak, piercing blue eyes, and sunlight-yellow feathers. His wings weren't leather but covered in feathers like an angel. His front talons were like bird legs, and if it wasn't for the draconic flank, he could've been easily mistaken for one giant bird.

Rocket had heard of other creatures known as 'griffons' and admitted that he resembled a griffon more than a dragon. But Drake insisted that he was just a different class of dragon. And who was Rocket to refute Drake?

Myst winced as Shiva's voice sounded from her mouth. *"So… who is this new… bird dragon? And why does he look so different from you?"*

Rocket chuckled at the confusion in her voice. "We're all special in our own way," she said. "Some of us control fire, others – like Swift here – wind. Luco loved how diverse he could make us…" She paused. For a moment, she almost forgot what Luco did.

Her scales glowed with her anger. Luco really took advantage of not just her, but all the other dragons: Blaze, Bang, even poor Swift. All they ever wanted to do was defend humans from the injustice Myst foisted upon them. That was what Luco made them for. Sure, Drake helped, but from what Rocket gathered, Luco had done most of the work.

Drake, Rocket could understand. He saw the demi-wolves as evil, and he acted. His speeches still echoed in her ears and her memories:

The demi-wolves are not more powerful than you, but they are more powerful than humans. More aggressive, and more intelligent. They don't have fear in their hearts for us, and they certainly don't have pity. Give them the chance, and they will massacre every man, woman, and child. You are our last hope to prevent this horrific fate.

She remembered Luco right behind him, nodding with a smile at his words. And yet… Luco made the demi-wolves. He knew better than anyone how they were just dogs, corrupted and hurt by his own hand. And yet he did nothing but nod and smile as Drake warned the dragons of how the demi-wolves were ruthless killers that had to be stopped.

Rocket looked back down the mountain to the towns and cities where humans dwelled. How many of them were like Luco? How many held evil in their hearts and were content to stand by and watch as suffering and torment ensued? Was it truly so appealing for humans to add to the world's pain rather than try to alleviate its suffering? Could… Rocket's scales glowed just thinking about it, but… could Drake be one of these bad humans?

"Hey, it's getting hot back here!" Myst barked, snapping Rocket back to the moment. Her scales cooled, and she eyed Swift in the distance.

"Regardless," Rocket continued. "Dragons were designed to be elemental. Some control fire, some control water. Swift controls wind. Not as strong as dragons like Blaze or myself, but he can fly better than any of us. And he can use that flight to watch everything going on in the world and let us know so we can act accordingly. He's our 'eye in the sky' so to speak."

Myst smirked. "Except for when wolves hide in the forests," she said. "Then your 'eye in the sky' has a much tougher time figuring out what we're up to."

"That's supposed to be over," Shiva interjected. *"Now that we're allies."*

Rocket grimaced but didn't protest. "Just let me do the talking," she warned. "You're not exactly popular with these guys."

"No, really?" Myst drawled. "I wouldn't have guessed."

"Oh, hush," Shiva grumbled, as Rocket flew towards Swift.

As Rocket drew closer, the wind dragon approached, his blue eyes wide and hopeful. "Rocket!" he said happily. "Did you get a new rider? Who's…"

Then he saw Myst's black fur. Her golden eyes. Swift froze in midair.

"Hang on," Rocket said, holding up Connors' amulet. "It's not what you think."

"W-What are you doing?" Swift demanded. "Why do you have that thing with you?"

Myst growled, but Rocket waved the nervous bird dragon off.

"I'm on orders from Connors," Rocket said. "And so is she." She glanced at Myst before looking back to Swift. "Have you seen Luco? Where's your Rider?"

"They're… talking," Swift admitted, jutting a talon back down the mountain. "Luco said he had some sort of grave warning." His feathers ruffled. "A warning about you."

Rocket's heart skipped a beat, but she maintained her composure. "I need to see him."

Swift looked uncertain, before flying back down the mountain.

Rocket followed after him but glanced at Myst worriedly. "He's not buying this," she muttered.

"Just let this play out," Myst recommended.

Soon enough, they reached a large nest, tucked into a cavern on the cliff face. Big enough for a couple of dragons to have shelter in. Luco was sitting right outside the cavern, alongside a human female in a Stetson hat. Blaze was nowhere to be seen, but Luco grinned as Swift, Rocket and Myst approached. Rocket tried to catch Myst's eyes, but the demi-wolf was locked on Luco with a fury Rocket knew very well. Luco's grin didn't fade, however. If anything, he looked like Rocket and Myst had impeccable timing.

"My-my, look at this. A wolf and a dragon, working together." Luco turned to the woman on his right, who's fingers were tracing a firearm strapped to her hip. "Isn't it just like I said?"

Swift looked to the woman in the Stetson like a child looking at their parent. "Rider Tex?" he asked. "What's going on?"

"I'm not sure," his rider admitted. "But you need to be ready, Swift." She looked up at Rocket. "Ignis-Drake R065; why do you have that thing on your back?"

Rocket's ears flattened as Swift glided to his rider's side. She quickly pulled up Connors' amulet, holding it out like a shield. "Swift, Tex, this wolf and I are on official business from King Connors."

Tex hummed, glaring past the amulet at Myst. "Didn't know Myst would let herself be put on a leash that easily."

"Don't push it, human," Myst growled. "Shiva may lead, but I haven't forgotten…"

"Quiet," Rocket growled, before she glared at Luco. "Rider Luco; you've refused to respond to the summons of King Connors. I'm here to escort you and Blaze back to Cadmus."

Swift blinked at Luco. "The King summoned you?"

"Swift," Tex barked, before glaring at Luco. "What's the King want with you?"

"Are you sure it's the King?" Luco asked. "Perhaps that's just what they want you to believe. So they can take me away and kill me in secret. The Roads are a dangerous place after all; it's so easy to have an 'accident' on those roads."

"Nothing's going to happen, as long as you cooperate," Rocket insisted.

"Like you? Cooperating with Myst?" Luco chuckled and looked at Swift and Tex, indicating Rocket and Myst. "Dear Rocket was made to protect humans, just like Swift. And yet, here she is, taking orders from the very monsters she was made to destroy, just like I warned you would happen."

"The only thing that's keeping you alive is Connors' directive," Myst said. "He wants to see you personally."

Swift's rider – Tex? – shook her head. "Hearing you talking about Connors' orders... it ain't sitting right with me."

"Exactly," Luco said triumphantly. "She's not really with Connors. She's just pretending to be. Surely, the leader of the demi-wolves wouldn't let anyone put a leash on her again."

Myst's claws dug into Rocket's scales. Rocket had to act.

"Not just her," Rocket said, before Myst could explode with rage. "We're both under orders from Connors." Her eyes narrowed. "And I haven't forgotten what you said back at the village."

Luco glanced at her with a bored expression.

"And you respond by working with terrorists?" he asked. "You're quite the petty lizard, aren't you?"

"Excuse me?" Tex demanded. "You turned for an argument, Rocket?"

"No!" Rocket insisted.

"You're the only terrorist here, human," Myst growled at Luco.

Myst's growl concerned Rocket. They needed to finish this, and quickly. "Enough of this," the dragon decided. She stepped forward and seized Luco.

Luco grabbed at her wrists. "Hey-hey!" he protested.

Tex went for her firearm but Myst snarled at her from Rocket's back. "Don't interfere, human," she warned.

Swift grabbed Tex and stepped back. Tex let him pull her back, though her glare didn't cease. Neither did her hold on her weapon.

"You're going to pay for the crimes you committed, Luco," Rocket said as she lifted Luco off the ground. "All the people you've hurt."

Suddenly, a growl made the earth rumble. The inside of the cavern lit up in yellow flames. Blaze stepped out, her normally pink eyes turning a dangerous red.

Myst rose up on Rocket's back in an attack posture, staying low and growling menacingly.

Swift yelped, taking to the air.

"Swift, hang on," Tex barked, climbing for his back. "I can get a shot on them as long as you stay in range."

"No-no, let him go," Luco called. "Spread the word! Rocket's gone rogue!"

Rocket seethed, but her eyes couldn't miss Swift, looking on her with so much fear.

Why are they so suspicious of me? Rocket thought. Having one of her fellow dragons gazing at her like she was Myst herself...

"I swear, Swift," Rocket called out. "You don't know what's really happening here."

"What's happening is that you're about to tear my face off," Luco noted.

"Don't listen to him, Rocket," Myst snapped. "He's tricking you!" She glared at Tex and Swift, the former of whom was aiming her firearm down at them. "Both of you!" She waved a claw at Luco. "He caused everything; he's been setting us up against each other when we should be focusing on him."

Luco rolled his eyes. "More pathetic justifications. Look, we all know the human race is flawed." He looked at Swift and Tex plaintively. "But does that really mean all of us have to die?"

"No," Tex said, while Swift nervously shook his head.

"Exactly." Luco turned back to Rocket. "Rider Tex here is a woman of principle. Of character." He grinned, as his voice dropped to a whisper. "A lot like Buck."

Fire burst from Rocket's scales – anger coursing through her veins.

"Rocket!" Myst barked.

But at that moment, Tex opened fire. Rocket and Myst jumped away from each other, letting the bullet pass between them, while Blaze came roaring out.

Just like when Blaze had first ambushed Rocket during her first confrontation with Luco.

Rocket threw Luco aside, caught Blaze's charge and rolled, redirecting the yellow dragon out of the nest and off the cliff. Blaze immediately took flight, while Rocket jumped back to her feet. Luco had already fled, pursued by Myst up a mountain trail.

"Luco!" Tex barked, forcing Swift to pursue them as she lined up a shot on Myst.

"No, Blaze will save me!" Luco promised. "You need to spread the word, Rider Tex! That's what Swift is for! Do not let anyone else be fooled by Rocket's lies! Tell them the truth before it's too late!"

"Shut it!" Myst barked, trying in vain to sink her claws into his flesh.

"Please, Tex," Swift said. "You said it yourself; I'm not meant for this kind of stuff. I'm not as strong as Blaze!"

Tex growled, glaring at Rocket as the dragon faced off with Blaze, before watching Myst close in on Luco. Spitting, Tex holstered her weapon.

"Alright, Swift," she said. "Let's go!"

Sighing in relief, Swift broke off from the chase and fled over the horizon, while Luco picked up his pace, Myst only pausing in brief confusion before continuing her pursuit.

"Myst, be careful!" Rocket roared, pumping her wings after the two. However, Blaze shot right by Rocket. And for once, Rocket didn't think to stop her.

Drake wanted Luco alive. If Myst killed him...

"Myst, please wait!" Rocket called, desperately trying to keep up with Blaze.

They found Luco approaching the summit of the mountain, Myst in hot pursuit. Blaze moved to the top, like she was ready to catch Luco…

And help him escape.

Despite her dark thoughts, hesitation still flared in Rocket's core: Blaze was her sister in arms. Her fellow dragon.

But she's also Luco's dragon. Can I really ask her to turn on him? Could I have turned on Buck?

Rocket's eyes narrowed in resolution. "Blaze, you can't do this!" Rocket insisted. "Luco's crazy. He needs to be captured!"

Blaze looked back and glowered at Rocket.

"Just let me help!" Rocket said, pumping her wings faster in an effort to keep up.

Blaze slowed. Her eyes faded to pink orbs of doubt. For a brief shining moment, Rocket thought she was listening.

Then Blaze's foot buried itself in Rocket's face. As she contorted in mid-air, Rocket felt Blaze's claws wrap around one of her wings.

CRACK!

Pain exploded across Rocket's back. She screamed as it felt like her wing had been torn off. And as Blaze released her, her tail lashed, knocking Rocket's head to the side and sending her plummeting back down the mountain.

For the first time in her life, terror shot through Rocket's gut. Her vision was fuzzy; her back stung with pain. She couldn't flap one of her wings; she had no idea if Blaze had just broken it or torn it out completely.

She turned bleary eyes up towards Blaze, flying back to the summit. Blaze's talons covered her mouth, as if she was horrified at what she had done. Blaze's wings started to tuck, like she wanted to dive after Rocket. But then Luco appeared, leaping off the top of the mountain and onto Blaze's back. Blaze paused, flapping backward as Myst appeared at the edge of the cliff seconds later, her golden eyes locking on Rocket's with horror.

"All actions have consequences, Misty," Luco mocked from the back of Blaze. "You can get one of us, but who are you gonna leave behind?"

"Go after him!" was what Rocket should have said. It would be so easy; all Myst had to do was jump onto Blaze. Myst already

hated Luco, and the maniac had his arms open, his neck exposed. It was perfect. And yet… Myst wanted to kill Luco. Would she really be able to bring him to justice?

Add to that, Rocket could feel the ground coming up. She was falling way too fast for the impact to be healthy. And with what felt like seconds left to live, she felt her heart screech out to both Blaze and Myst, *"No, save me! Please, I don't want to die!"*

With one disgusted glare at Luco, Myst jumped… and dove after Rocket.

"You fool!" Rocket's brain screamed.

She could hear Luco laughing. Saw Blaze reach out for her before he grabbed her spines.

"Quick Blazy, go!"

Reluctantly, Blaze jetted away. There wasn't a way for Myst to catch Rocket in time, and Swift was long gone. No one was going to be able to help her.

But she underestimated the strength of the pack link. As Myst's fur once again lit up, a pack link tendril coursed out of her claws and clung to Rocket's chest like a spider web.

"Help her!" Myst's voice boomed through her head.

"*Transferring energy now,*" Shiva's voice responded.

Rocket felt a surge of energy shoot through her – like the time Buck had fed her the dreaded Ghost Peppers. She remembered what Buck told her when she first started flying.

"*Relax your wings. Extend and glide.*"

Obeying his instruction, Rocket extended her wings, and… they caught the air.

Rocket turned, her eyes wide and her jaw agape. The wing that Blaze had damaged was whole again! It was like Blaze had never even touched it! Unfortunately, even as Rocket managed to pull out of her fall, Myst landed hard on her back. They hit the mountain side and tumbled down the incline - dragon over demi-wolf. Luckily, there was an exposed shelf to stop their slide. They came to a rest, bloodied, and bruised, but not broken.

"Ow…" Rocket moaned.

"Easy does it," Myst said. "Shiva?"

"*I'm already on it,*" Shiva's voice whispered.

Rocket felt the bruises on her body begin to fade. The ringing in her head lessened. But even as her body healed, she couldn't help but look up and watch as Blaze and her psychotic rider disappeared over the horizon.

"Teeth-For-Days' Fangs," Rocket swore. "We had him!" She looked to Myst. "What was Shiva thinking?"

"That wasn't Shiva," Myst replied. "That was all me."

Rocket blinked, uncomprehending. "Why?"

Myst's gaze was determined. "Because in the pack, we take care of each other. That's the promise. And unlike humans like Luco, we keep our promises."

Rocket hung her head in shame. "But you would've caught him if it wasn't for me."

"It's not over yet," Shiva's voice warned. *"We still have his scent. Myst can still track him."*

"Exactly," Myst agreed, though her voice wavered in confidence.

Rocket sighed, shifting into a sitting position as the last of the pain left her.

"I'd have been dead if it wasn't for that demi-wolf," Rocket realized, glancing at Myst. "Myst..."

The demi-wolf looked back at her dragon partner. "Huh?"

Rocket tried to say something… a 'thank you,' or an 'I appreciate your aid'… but at the same time, she couldn't help but think of how she could've caught Luco. And as frustration flooded her veins, she found herself remembering all the other things Myst had done over the years. Glancing down at the pack link still bound to her chest, she severed it with a swipe of her talons.

Myst gazed down at the broken pack link in confusion. "What is it, Rocket?" she asked.

Rocket glared at her. Was she being coy or something? It was hard to tell with the demi-wolf.

Rocket shook her head and waved Myst off. "We need a better plan." She turned away, while intrusive thoughts circled her like a vulture.

I just got rescued by Myst herself! A dragon owes her life to the creature that should be her mortal enemy.

We're zero for two… What are we going to do?

Even though Myst was miles away from her home and sanctuary, when she shut her eyes and concentrated, the pack link brought her to a mental manifestation of the forest.

Of course, it wasn't perfect: for some reason, the soft earth and trees were always blanketed with snow, even when the sky was blue and bright above them. Maybe Shiva preferred it that way, or the experience was just naturally like that. Myst wasn't sure, but she didn't know how to change it, and she didn't have the time to worry about it.

Especially now, with Luke and Shiva walking out of the light to meet with her. Though Shiva and Luke looked sympathetic, Myst couldn't share in their sympathy. She glared down as her memories formed before them: Luco grinning at Myst from Blaze's back, Rocket plummeting to her death below them.

"All actions have consequences, Misty," Luco had mocked. *"You can get one of us, but who are you gonna leave behind?"*

Myst shook her head as, in the memory, she dove after Rocket.

"How is she?" Shiva asked, swiping the image away. "She cut the link on me shortly after her vitals were restored."

"She's meeting with General Drake," Myst said. "He's not going to be happy about this."

Luke tsked. "Can't believe I'm feeling bad for a dragon."

Myst's glower, however, didn't fade. "I could've gotten him. I had him in my sights and I let him go."

"You kept a vow," Shiva assured her. "Like you mentioned, it's important to show why we can be trusted."

Luke grimaced as Myst's memory of Swift flying away appeared. "I don't think that dragon was convinced."

"Luco got into the dragon's mind," Myst said. "Him and his rider." Her ears perked. "If he turns the other dragons against Rocket…"

"Drake should be able to stop that," Shiva insisted. "He's the Alpha."

"He should, but what if he can't?"

"We can't control that," Shiva said. "We can only control how we react to it." She paused, considering. "Speaking of which, how's it going with Rocket?"

They gazed down at the memories: Rocket sitting isolated and defeated as the pack link worked to heal her physical wounds.

"I'd have been dead if it wasn't for that demi-wolf," her thoughts echoed. She sounded so confused. Like it shouldn't have happened; like her world view had just been thrown into question.

"She's interesting," Myst admitted. "I was familiar with the dragon's upbringing: how they were raised to be fighters; guardians that destroy anything that threatens their charges. But it's another thing to see how devoted she is. Luco's very existence - his sociopathic tendencies? His ability to use the things they believe in to turn them against each other? It stands against everything she's ever known. And I'm not sure she's capable of handling it."

Shiva looked away. "Losing her Rider probably didn't help," she commented.

Luke and Myst exchanged worried looks. "Shiva," Luke said softly. "You didn't have a choice."

Shiva turned back. But before she could speak…

"What choice?"

The group turned to find a golden wolf pup trying to join them.

"Celine?" Shiva chided. "What did I say; you have chores to do."

"But Kodo wanted to see…" Celine started to say, before silver pack threads pulled her back into the shadows.

"No, Celine, sh!" Kodo hissed, wincing as his parents and Myst glared at him. He chuckled sheepishly, before retreating into the shadows. Celine didn't follow her brother, gazing up at Shiva and Luke in confusion.

Luke chuckled, while Shiva just sighed. The couple looked to each other.

"Your turn?" Shiva asked.

"My turn," Luke replied with a grin. He glanced at Myst. "You can do this, Myst. Try not to murder each other while I'm gone."

Myst scoffed, indignant. But she couldn't keep herself from grinning as Luke hefted Celine up like a bag of flour, and faded from the link. Shiva shut her eyes, her own quiet grin playing across her face.

"You do a good job with them," Myst noted. "They're going to be great Alphas one day."

Shiva smiled softly at Myst's words, before shaking away her sentiment.

"Don't lose focus," she insisted. "Luco needs to be brought in. Whatever he's planning to do with the other dragons... we need a plan to catch him before he infects any more minds."

Not questioning the change in subject, Myst nodded. "I think the humans might have something. I'll go find out."

Shiva nodded, and let the pack link fade out.

With Myst's head back in the present, she turned to rejoin Rocket. Drake paced before the dragon, Connors and Fawkes stood further back.

"'Rocket's gone rogue,'" Drake growled. "'Rocket's gone rogue.' That's all that Swift is saying, and he's been spreading it across every village we have in the East District!" He turned to Connors. "C-Your Majesty, it was bad enough when Luco dragged Rocket in front of me, saying how she destroyed a man's home. Now Swift is spreading the word that she's working with Myst? A sigil from you isn't going to protect her!"

Myst paused in walking up next to Rocket, though when the dragon glanced at her, eyes filled with doubt, Myst found herself standing supportively beside her.

Despite Myst's support, Rocket's gaze cast back downward.

Myst grimaced. She hated this hesitation and distrust between them. She was used to a pack that trusted, obeyed, and looked up to her.

Myst chuckled darkly; Shiva and Rocket would get along great with each other, had things gone differently between them.

"So," Connors noted, grabbing Myst's attention. "What did Shiva have to say?"

Myst glanced at Rocket. "We're questioning the validity of this alliance. Drake and Luco have trained the dragons so thoroughly, that their loyalty to both of them is unquestioned."

Rocket gave Myst a dirty look. "Loyalty isn't a bad thing…"

"Until it's being used to manipulate and hide the truth from others," Myst countered. She looked to Connors. "I'm not sure if the dragon can do this job."

Connors glanced at Drake. "Then why was Rocket willing to give demi-wolves a chance."

Rocket flinched, while Myst crossed her arms.

"You could've killed Shiva when you found her," Connors pointed out. "And instead, you brought her back."

"She had the pack link," Rocket protested. "She had an ability no wolf had shown before!"

"Was that all?" Connors asked with a knowing grin. "Or was there a part of you that empathized with her? A part of you that realized she was just a scared child and didn't deserve to die?"

Rocket looked away, shaking her head. "I... it wasn't..."

Drake walked over to Rocket, touching her side. "You did the right thing, Rocket," he assured her. "Bringing her to me; making me aware of her powers... Don't think that wasn't the right move to make." He glared at Connors. "Unfortunately, if you continue to spin it as her being sympathetic, her reputation is going to take a dive."

"And it's only going to get worse the longer Luco is allowed to roam free," Connors replied, turning his gaze to Rocket and Myst. "We need to come up with a plan for you two."

Myst nodded. "Well, I almost had Luco until he escaped on Blaze. Back when we fought with you guys, our standard strategy was to separate the riders from their dragons and take them on individually."

Drake tensed. "Let me remind you that you were ordered to bring them both in alive."

"And we will," Myst replied. "It just has to be separately. First, we bring in Blaze. Then, without her to cart Luco around and defend him, the maniac should follow shortly afterward."

Rocket perked up. "Blaze didn't look happy about fighting me. And she didn't hear what Luco said. Maybe if we separate them, we can convince her why she has to come back. And if we can convince her of the truth…"

"She'll make a formidable ally," Connors mused.

Drake didn't look convinced, but Connors smiled. "Then it sounds like you have a plan. Track Luco down, and when you find him, focus on capturing Blaze first."

Drake grimaced. "Just don't forget to bring her in alive. Blaze is still your sister, Rocket. And you can't afford to prove Luco right about you."

"I won't forget, General," Rocket promised. "Humans will always take priority. Even over my own life."

Myst stared at her in shock. She noticed Drake grimacing, equally uncomfortable with Rocket over-eager altruism. But neither of them had time to vocalize their points.

"Then hurry," Connors said. "Time runs short."

Myst climbed onto Rocket, and they took to the sky, heading back towards the east. It was a bright day, and the sun – high in the sky – felt warm even as Myst felt the coolness of the wind. Yet, even in the air, Myst watched Rocket with conflict.

"What was that about?" Myst asked.

"Huh?"

"All humans take priority even over your own life? Did Drake seriously tell you that?"

"I've been taught that from the moment I came out of my egg," Rocket said.

"Well," Myst noted. "My experience is that all humans are vicious and unreliable."

"And that's why you're the enemy," Rocket said.

"We need to move beyond that," Myst insisted. "We're not enemies anymore. The enemy is the person trying to destroy our way of life. And that happens to be a human named Luco." Myst paused, before admitting, "Shiva has managed to teach me – however reluctant I am to admit it – that some humans do have goodness in them. If I can learn to accept the virtues in humanity, why can't you acknowledge their vices?"

"Why would I need to learn that?" Rocket demanded.

"Look at what happened," Myst insisted, indicating her wing. "You gave Luco and Blaze the benefit of the doubt, and you were almost killed for it."

Rocket stiffened. "That was a mistake. One I won't repeat." She glared at Myst. "If I get into trouble like that, you don't go back for me. Just…"

"No, it's not about me going back for you, it's about 'why' I had to in the first place! You can't use your power effectively as long as you continue to give Luco the benefit of the doubt."

"I can't just mindlessly kill him like an animal!" Rocket protested.

Myst kept herself calm. "I'm not asking you to do that. I'm asking you to recognize that he is the enemy. And that if we don't beat him, a lot more people will die. Not just you."

Rocket looked down with a glower, before sighing. "Can you track him?"

"Of course." She pointed. "Keep going this way."

Rocket nodded, and increased the flames propelling her. However, before long...

"Myst," Rocket said, giving the demi-wolf pause. "I-If he forces us to choose again... if I can't stop myself from... I..."

Myst looked back at her. "You want me to prioritize capturing him... but at the same time, another part of you doesn't want to die."

Rocket lowered her head. Myst made Rocket look at her.

"It's like I said," Myst said. "In the wolf pack, we sacrifice for each other all the time. But it's our duty to still look after each other. When one wolf takes a hit for another, the other wolf will do their best to help the one who helped them. That's the choice we make. And as Shiva taught me, it doesn't matter if that choice is made by a wolf or a dragon or even a human. What matters is that someone made that choice to help rather than hurt. Luco has made choices that are hurting us and the ones we love. If you can recognize that, then we can work together. And together, we can take him down."

Rocket's lips curled in a half-smile. She turned to the horizon with newfound confidence.

"Then let's keep going," she said. "The next time we find Luco, Blaze is going down."

Myst tilted her head. "Well, since we left Drake, I've been wondering: when we were at war, my main concern was trying to kill you guys. I honestly have no idea how we'd capture one of you alive."

Rocket narrowed her eyes. "Luckily for you, I've got a few ideas."

Chapter 7

As Myst's nose led them through the eastern villages, they came across a fishing town adjacent to a large river. It was early morning; the docks were bustling with fishermen heading out to sea or working on equipment. A few faces turned upward as Rocket circled the town. Some of them waved to Rocket... while others pointed. Concerned, Rocket made sure her wings were spread so that people couldn't notice Myst that well. With the plan she and Myst developed brewing in her mind, she didn't have it in her to deal with people panicking or worrying about Myst attacking them.

After all, what did they know about Myst? What did they know about the soul that dwelled underneath that fur and those claws?

Rocket suddenly second-guessed herself. *"She's guilty of crimes against humanity, and I'm one of the dragons created to stop her. Everything about this partnership feels wrong!"*

And yet, a voice in her head noted. *How else are we going to beat Luco and save Blaze?*

"Where are these conflicting thoughts coming from," she mused. Briefly, she looked back at Myst – suspecting Shiva was using the pack link on her. But Myst's fur was dim; the pack link was apparently dormant. Myst's eyes scanned the ground as Rocket circled over the town. And when she spoke, it was out loud.

"I was just thinking," Myst noted. "Since you've got fire power… does Drake have you cook meat or things for him?"

Rocket blinked. "You cook meat?"

Myst smiled. "Before we became demi-wolves, no. But once we became demi-wolves, we got a few advantages. You're saying you never considered using your fire for more mundane tasks?"

Rocket scoffed. "That's like trying to start a campfire with a stick of dynamite. Someone could get hurt."

Myst nodded. "Ah, yes, and all life is precious."

Rocket narrowed her eyes. "That sounds like sarcasm."

"No, I'm serious." Myst assured. "I hate humans, not all forms of life. And while Shiva's pack link does increase our hunting abilities, she's made it very clear that what we fight or hunt are living creatures in their own right. So, we honor them. We give the prey the respect it deserves."

Rocket rolled her eyes. "Doesn't stop you from killing them."

"It's the balance of nature," Myst insisted. "We don't take more than we can eat. If there are too many plant-eaters, they'll destroy the forests, right?" She lifted a claw. "One thing Shiva's peace taught me is that it goes both ways as well: if we kill too many of them, and our own numbers grow too big, we'll all die out just the same. Everything's got to be in balance."

"So what?" Rocket asked. "You think you're... helping the planet by hurting those creatures?"

"Hurting's the wrong word. It's no different than the hunt we're making for Luco, or those fishermen going out to catch fish. We don't have to kill Luco... even though I really want to. But sometimes, you have to be willing to do some unpleasant things in order to achieve some good. Some balance."

Rocket's glare faltered, and she watched as some of the fishermen close to shore cast out their nets. "I guess," Rocket said. "It's just hard for me to not feel like you're..." she paused in thought, as she slowly circled towards the town square. "You've cleaned up your act, don't get me wrong, but it still feels like the same dark brutality underneath."

Myst sighed. "Well, what do you want me to say? That the humans aren't all bad? Look at Luco! Wanna try and tell me how he's a saint?"

"I know he isn't…" Rocket growled. "I've had to deal with my General and my King telling me that my rider – my best friend – deserved to die." Before Myst could speak, Rocket looked away, focusing on landing. "A-And I don't know if he did or not. Luco's thrown my whole view of the world into question now, and…"

Her thoughts were interrupted by a scream. "MYST!"

Rocket turned to the source, two humans watching them with wide eyes.

"It's like Luco said," one of the humans cried. "Myst's got a dragon. We're doomed!"

Rocket's eyes narrowed. "Luco's been lying to you. He's the enemy, not us!"

"That's exactly what a minion of Myst might say," the other human yelled, picking up a stone to throw.

A crowd was gathering. Rocket reached for Connors' sigil around her neck, even as she feared it would do little good.

"People," she said. "You have to listen to me…"

"Watch it," Myst said, pulling her back just as a stone sailed past her snout. Rocket turned to the thrower, her flames licking at her lips.

"KNOCK IT OFF!" she barked, flames spitting from her jaws and sending the stone-thrower scrambling back.

"SEE? Luco told us she's dangerous!"

Rocket held her head with a frustrated growl. But before she could try to explain or Myst could cut in…

"TRAITOR!" a larger, more powerful voice boomed.

Rocket and Myst turned just as a wet blob of blue launched from the docks and splashed into Rocket. Rocket and Myst were knocked apart, sprawling across the wet cobblestone as the crowd ran screaming.

"What the…? Jackknife?!"

The Pack Link flared to life around Myst as she pulled herself up. Rocket wondered what Shiva would think of the newest dragon to challenge them; a scaly serpent a little bigger than a man.

His body was made of water, allowing Rocket to spy his rider, coated in pulsing, gel like liquid that covered him like a suit of armor. The water formed a snake-like head, and despite standing on legs like man, a long tail like a dolphin smacked the ground behind him.

"Jack, Bai Long, you..." Rocket struggled to ignite her fire with her scales soaked. "What are you doing?"

"Stay outta this, Rocket," the human said from inside his water-snake-like helm. "Luco warned me that Myst was up to her old tricks."

"He said she brainwashed ya," the snake helm spoke, in a husky voice far different from his rider. "Making ya cavort wid wolves and plan to hurt humans. And look what we find ya doing?!"

Rocket tried to avoid looking at the crowd. "There's a reasonable explanation for that..." She tried to lift Connors sigil, but...

"Luco's deceiving you," Myst said. "We're here to..."

"I don't wanna hear it!" the dragon hissed. "Have at ya!" He charged... only for Rocket to intercept him.

Rocket recalled what she remembered about Jackknife – born with control over water instead of fire. Since Drake seemed to prefer the fire dragons over the others, it had given Jackknife an annoying inferiority complex that made negotiating with him difficult. It didn't help his attitude that his true form was smaller than that of a fire dragon – looking more like a dog-sized sea horse than a full-sized dragon. Instead of Li Bai Long – Jackknife's Rider - riding Jackknife, Jackknife rode Bai Long.

But wait, Rocket realized. He was only powerful when he was with his rider. If she could just separate the two, she'd negate his power. And if she could remember the strike correctly…

Her fist caught Bai Long in the chest, and Jackknife's true form was knocked from his rider's back.

Got it, Rocket thought.

Working in concert with Rocket's tact, Myst snatched Jackknife out of the air, jumping onto Rocket while the watery armor burst like a popped balloon, leaving his rider Bai Long soaked and defenseless. The pack link encircled Jackknife, securing him, while Rocket turned back to the crowd.

"Jackknife!" the rider called.

"Li!" the water dragon cried, only to gag.

Myst snarled, baring her teeth as she squeezed Jackknife's body.

"Myst, hold on a moment!" Rocket warned.

"Don't worry," Myst said. "Nothing's gonna happen... as long as Jackknife here doesn't pull anything."

Jackknife squirmed in defiance, but Bai Long raised his hands. "Whoa, take it easy," he insisted. "Rocket, please... don't let her hurt him."

"Don't worry, buddy," Jackknife said. "I won't give up!" He glared at Rocket. "I don't care how weird you've gotten, Rocket! You and Myst'll never win! De humans will survive and endure! De dragons will protect!"

"They will," Rocket assured him. "But you're fighting the wrong enemy. You have to listen to us." She turned to Li as he started to approach. "You too, Bai Long; hold on a moment."

Jackknife didn't respond, trying to pull himself out from Myst's grip. Myst's fur glowed with the pack link, and Myst's ears flicked like Shiva was telling her something.

"Shiva wants to try and get through to him with the link," Myst explained.

Rocket grimaced. "Jack…" she tried to say.

"Do yer worst!" Jackknife snarled at her. "I'll never give up!"

"What do you think you're doing?" Bai Long demanded.

Rocket sighed. She could feel the stares of everyone around them. But before Myst could let Shiva use her pack link…

"You see?!" a familiar voice cried. "One of our great dragons tries to stop them, and they're about to torture him to death! Oh, the inhumanity!"

"Luco!" Rocket and Myst growled, turning to find Luco pointing his finger at them. Blaze rose up behind Luco, growling at them with red eyes.

"Quick, everyone!" Luco said. "Flee for your lives! Rocket here has turned her back on humanity. She sees us all as evil now, worthy of burning in the fiery pits of Tartarus!"

Rocket seethed, before another voice spoke out.

"But… that's Connors' sigil around her neck."

Rocket looked for the source, and smiled as she spotted a familiar dreadlocked ponytail. *Fawkes.*

"The King wouldn't just give that out to anyone!" Fawkes insisted. "Maybe there's more to this than we realize."

"No, she's working with Myst!" another cried. "She clearly can't be trusted!"

"But we've done nothing but trust the dragons!" another voice protested. "Can't we give them some faith?"

"Yeah, I know Rocket," another voice said. "She's always been a protector. She has to have a good reason."

"No reason justifies working with Myst!"

As the crowd began to argue back and forth, Rocket, Myst, Bai Long and even Jackknife paused in their fight to watch them. Luco's grin faded as the people argued and even a few fist fights broke out.

Luco waved his arms at the crowd. "Wait; no need to fear, ladies and gentlemen," he said. "My fearless dragon Blaze will put an end to this traitor and save our courageous Jackknife."

"I don't need saving!" Jackknife roared. "Dey need saving from me!"

But Luco ignored him, turning to Blaze. "Blaze, defend the humans."

Myst and Rocket turned to each other. Jackknife was still wriggling in Myst's grip, but Shiva's pack link was tied around him.

"Shiva's got the water dragon," Myst whispered. "Remember; we get Blaze first. I'll give Luco a good scare so he doesn't know what we're up to."

With Blaze bearing down on them, Rocket had no time for anything but nodding and saying, "You got it."

With Jackknife curled under her arm, Myst leaped off Rocket to confront Luco, while Rocket squared off with Blaze, Bai Long diving for cover. Though her last two losses had been painful and humiliating, Rocket was determined not to make this zero and three. Catching Blaze's charge and redirecting her away from Myst and Jackknife, Rocket sparred with her bigger counterpart, avoiding her powerful grip and delivering a series of fire-enshrouded jabs to Blaze's side and head.

"You're on the wrong side, sis," Rocket said as she fought. "Help us against Luco."

"Liar," Blaze hissed, fire spitting from her maw and forcing Rocket back.

But Rocket closed the distance. "I can't let you get away a third time."

"You see?!" Luco continued to cry out as he and the crowd fled from Myst. "Taking a demi-wolf's orders? Working with her avowed enemies?! Traitor! Renegade!"

"Will you shut up!" Fawkes cried out, throwing a bola at him.

"For once, I agree!" Myst snarled, lunging at Luco as he dodged Fawkes' attack… only for Bai Long to tackle her from behind. As the human got Myst to the ground, Jackknife popped free of Myst's grip. Bai Long seized Jackknife from the air, and the second they made contact, the watery armor reformed around Jackknife and his rider. The pack link still glowed around them as Shiva tried to convince Jackknife of their innocence. But Jackknife's eyes were narrowed, and he fought against the pack link.

"Won't… let you… trick me," he hissed.

"Jack?" Bai Long asked. "What's going on, brother?"

"Nothing to worry about," Jackknife assured him. "Just keep Myst away from de people."

"I'm not the threat," Myst growled, backing up and glancing towards Fawkes and Luco. The King's bodyguard chased after Luco, barraging him with bolas as he leaped from cover to cover. "Hey, what happened to not harming him?" Myst shouted to Fawkes.

"These won't harm him?" Fawkes replied. "Much."

"That's too much for me," Luco said. "BLAZE!"

Blaze dodged a strike from Rocket and rolled past her, catching Myst with a lash from her tail.

The poor demi-wolf crashed into a building and vanished under a pile of rubble as the pack link faded from Jackknife's body.

Yet, Luco wasn't satisfied. "NOT HER, THE HUMAN! STOP THE HUMAN WHO'S CHASING ME!"

Blaze froze, and even Jackknife paused to stare at Luco. "You kidding?" Jackknife asked.

"She's trying to break my neck with bolas!" Luco insisted.

"Uh… why?" Bai Long asked.

Fawkes smiled. "I'm glad you asked." She turned to the group, only for Luco to rush at her with his club.

Rocket leaped to defend Fawkes, only to be forced to dodge when Blaze jumped to Luco's defense. Grimacing, Rocket dodged Blaze's strikes, and answered back with a lash from her own tail, only for Jackknife to catch her off guard with a blast of water. And though his water evaporated against her, it quenched her flames.

Rocket seethed in rage, catching Jackknife's fist and redirecting it into Blaze. For a brief moment, the two dragons staggered, and Rocket got a chance to rest. Out of the corner of her eye, she saw Myst struggling out of the rubble, her fur shining as Shiva healed her. Myst's eyes darted between Rocket and Luco, as the latter rapidly retreated from Fawkes' attack.

"Myst, remember our plan!" Rocket reminded her, before Jackknife and Blaze recovered.

"Stop de wolf!" Jackknife ordered Blaze. "I got de traitor."

Blaze nodded, shifting her focus to the demi-wolf while Jackknife came for Rocket.

Rocket tried not to grin. Blaze thought she was defeating Myst. But what she didn't know was that Myst's Pack Link would allow her to drain Blaze's fire and weaken her enough to defeat.

As long as Jackknife and Luco didn't interfere.

With her plan on her mind, Rocket redirected Jackknife into a store stall, where he seemed to explode, before reforming and deluging her in another blast of water. Rocket's fire dimmed further as she sought to reignite herself.

She had to endure. She needed to get Jackknife away from Blaze and Myst long enough for Shiva to weaken Blaze. And to do that, she needed to get some distance.

Knowing Jackknife couldn't fly, she took to the air. It was difficult without her fire to give her a boost, but Rocket pumped her wings harder, and was able to get some altitude and distance as Jackknife continued to throw water at her.

Off to the side, Rocket spotted Myst and Blaze. The demi-wolf was circling the fire dragon, her pack link shining as she slowly but surely tied Blaze up. The dragon furiously blasted flames in every direction, trying to hit Myst and break the pack link. Further away, Luco was leaving town, Fawkes encouraging his exit with a seemingly unlimited number of bolas.

Rocket was almost amazed. Their plan was working. Now, if she could just keep Jackknife from interfering a little longer...

"I don't want to hurt you, Jack," she warned. "There's a lot going on here you don't understand."

Jackknife hissed in fury. "You fire dragons dink yer so tough!" he spat. "Always getting de glory cuz fire's flashier dan water. Well, let's see how flashy you are after a good soak!"

He lifted his arms towards the river, and globs of water shot from the body of water, pelting at Rocket like inverse rain.

Rocket tucked her wings and dove into town, dodging the barrage, just as Blaze got in a lucky shot with her tail.

Tripping Myst off her paws, Blaze seized the pack link threads in her jaws and spun, hurling Myst like a morning star towards one of the buildings.

Remembering how the pack link had faded the last time, Rocket swooped in low and tight. She caught Myst with her chest, and as the demi-wolf sunk into her scales, Rocket felt a jolt of power as the pack link twined around her, and Blaze's power surged into Rocket.

Blaze chewed valiantly on the threads, but the magic links refused to break. Add to that, Blaze's fire began to dim, and her legs collapsed out from under her as the pack link drained her. Jackknife laughed as the yellow dragon floundered.

"Wassa matter, fire dragon," he asked. "Can't get out without help? Don't worry; I gotcha."

He clenched his fists, looking like he was trying to lift a building. And the water in the river responded, rising like a tidal wave over the town.

Rocket's eyes bugged out of her skull. "Are you insane, Jackknife?! You'll flood the town! You'll kill everyone."

Some people in the crowd overheard. "She... is trying to protect us?"

Jackknife faltered, looking back.

"Jackknife," Bai Long said. "Don't. She's right; you'd destroy the town. Don't let your pride make you do something you will regret."

"But..." Jackknife mumbled, shrinking down. "She's..."

"I am trying to protect you guys, Jackknife," Rocket promised. "All I want is to stop Luco."

Jackknife paused, frowning in conflict. Bai Long, however, gently lowered the water dragon's arms, and the great wave subsided.

Rocket nodded in thanks. "Keep the people here safe," she said. Depositing Myst on her back, she gathered up the pack link threads. With Blaze's power coursing through her and her fire reignited she was able to lift the trussed-up dragon almost effortlessly.

"Alright, Myst," Rocket said. "I've got her. Let's go."

Myst nodded. "Nice job… pack mate."

Rocket grinned. "You too… Rider."

Myst wasn't sure what to think of Blaze's incarceration. For her and the demi-wolves, dragons were their most hated foes; to see one beaten was more than a mark of victory. It was a sign of hope; of power and the belief that they could actually defeat the tyrannical humans.

But the way Blaze was contained now: moved from the pier to a secure jail cell, up to her neck in a tank of ice water, the steam and boiling bubbles hiding the chains that bound her talons, tail and wings, and the muzzle that glowed bright red against her snout. There was something... sad about it. Sure, Blaze had tried to kill Rocket and Myst, and yet... it reminded Myst of the dog pounds. The lines of cages where dogs and other animals had been locked up, denied freedom, and treated like cattle.

No creature deserves this kind of fate.

And yet, they were doing it to Blaze. Myst couldn't help but feel a squirming sensation in her gut.

Shiva and the others might find this amusing, no doubt. I can watch a thousand humans die without flinching, but put one of us in a cage, and suddenly, I'm squeamish. She huffed. *Well maybe they should all realize that the cage is but one fate I consider worse than death!*

Blaze didn't seem terrified, though. She sat casually in her cell, watching General Drake as he paced before her with a disappointed expression. Aside from some prominent sweat on his forehead, the heat didn't seem to be affecting the General. His fire-colored eyes stared at Blaze's, but her pink eyes didn't falter.

"What's Luco planning?" the General asked. "What does he have to gain from this madness?"

Blaze was silent. The steam hissed around her jaws, and the water boiled from her body heat.

Drake sighed. "Look, I know he's your Rider and he means a lot to you. But surely you should have drawn the line somewhere. His antics cost human lives and threatened many more."

Blaze grimaced and looked away, but still didn't speak.

"I know you normally don't speak, but that water will keep you from accidentally breathing flames on me. So, as your General, I am ordering you to tell me what he's planning."

Blaze still didn't meet his gaze. For a moment, Drake glared at the bound dragon. His eyes glanced towards the two-way mirror, where Myst, Rocket, Connors, and his bodyguard Fawkes were watching. Myst didn't say anything, but the dark demi-wolf could feel Shiva and Luke watching through the pack link as well.

Finally, Drake huffed. "Fine," he growled. "We'll do this the hard way." He turned and walked out. Blaze didn't even flinch when he slammed the door.

Rocket shook her head as Drake entered the observation room.

"Son of a she-dog," he muttered.

"Hey," Myst growled.

"You do have to admit, Myst," Connors said. "That was rather disappointing."

"With all due respect," Drake replied. "Blaze has always been Luco's girl. He picked her almost the instant her egg was made. And she never seemed to have a thought for herself."

"Something's going on with her," Rocket said. "And we need to find out what it is." She cracked her knuckles. "Maybe she'll respond to some full-contact sparring."

Drake sighed. "No. You know that won't work, Rocket; I raised you girls on fighting. At worst, you'll give her a chance to break loose."

Myst stepped forward. "What about the pack link?"

Drake tensed. "I don't like your magic near my dragons."

"Then why do we have her here?" Connors refuted. He turned to Myst. "If you believe Shiva can help, then I'm willing to give it a chance. Just... don't hurt her, okay?"

Myst narrowed her eyes at the human, before sparing a glance at Rocket. Rocket shook her head gently, silently asking for Myst not to get confrontational. With a sigh, Myst nodded. Rocket smiled.

"It'll be okay, General," Rocket assured Drake. "Myst has been true to her word so far."

Drake looked back at Blaze, before sighing. "Yeah. Because I'll make sure of it." He turned to Myst. "If you're going to do this, then I want to be in there with you. I want to make sure nothing bad happens to my dragon."

Myst held back a retort, and nodded. Together, the General and the demi-wolf walked out of the observation room, and into the interrogation room.

The heat hit Myst like a wall; the humidity dampening the air until it felt like she was trying to breath while swimming underwater. For a moment, she stood at the door, and just let the room air out.

Drake grinned at her discomfort. "Too hot for you."

Myst ignored the General, and followed him inside.

Blaze's eyes turned red at the sight of Myst, and she pushed back against her tank. The water splashed and boiled as Blaze's body heat increased, and her straining worsened as the pack link spiraled to life around Myst.

"I warned you," Drake noted. "We could've done this easy, but you picked the hard way."

"I know you don't trust me," Myst said. "But I'm really not here to hurt you."

Blaze just glowered at Myst; her expression one of mocking contempt.

"We have to find a way to stop Luco," Myst said, as the pack link tendrils crept towards Blaze. "Try to relax."

"No funny business," Drake warned, before taking one of the tendrils, watching it carefully as it wrapped around his dragon tattoo.

Blaze jerked her head away, trying as best she could to delay the pack link grabbing her. But with her restraints, there was little she could do, and the tendrils bound around her snout. With a flash of light, the three found themselves back in the white clearing of the mind link.

Blaze stood in the middle of the clearing. She looked around, blinking in confusion, before her eyes returned to Myst and Drake, grimacing as Shiva's form materialized between them.

"Welcome to the Pack Link," Shiva noted with a grin.

Blaze growled and shot fire at the two wolves, but it passed harmlessly through them.

Drake chuckled darkly. "That's my girl." Shiva's grin faded.

"Nice to see you too," Shiva deadpanned.

Myst looked around. "Where's Luke?"

"He's trying to spend time with the kids," Shiva replied, earning a raised eyebrow from Drake and even Blaze.

"You got pups already?" Drake mused. He looked away. "Well, you've been busy, haven't you?" he muttered under his breath.

Myst huffed, but the idea of interrupting Kodo's time with his father was enough to get her to stand down, as Shiva approached Blaze under the watchful eye of Drake.

"You aided an anarchist in torture," she said to Blaze. "Rocket said you were made to protect human life, and yet you have contributed to their suffering instead. You helped Luco send humans at our borders to die or provoke our wrath, and now your assistance has resulted in the dragons turning on each other." Shiva narrowed her eyes. "Why?"

Blaze snorted, and looked away. Shiva sighed, and her fur glowed. But instead of memories forming before them, Shiva only got images of fire. Her brow furrowed, before Myst noticed Blaze smirking.

"Your mental tricks aren't gonna work," Blaze whispered. "Luco protected me against them. He'll come for me soon enough." Her grin widened. "And anything you do to me, he'll unleash on you tenfold."

Myst's fur bristled. She stepped forward, scraping her claws against each other.

"Myst…" Drake warned, but she ignored him.

"Let him come then," Myst sneered. "After everything he's already put me through, I'll barely feel it. Unlike you."

"Hey," Drake said, getting between them. "I just warned you, no funny business."

"I agree!" Shiva said. "If Luco's planned for this, then digging into her mind will only hurt us. So, calm down."

Myst growled, fuming internally at the smug look Blaze shot her. "He mutates me into a monster," Myst snarled. "Manipulated us into war, and now has altered your mind?" She glared up at Blaze. "How can you be okay with this?"

Blaze held her head high. "He's my Rider," she insisted. "He's my Father." She paused for a small moment, before adding, "He loves me."

Myst's temper snapped. She lunged at Blaze, barely able to contain herself when Shiva barked, "Stand down! If you can't control yourself…"

"A MONSTER LIKE THAT CAN'T LOVE!" Myst yelled. "Where was his love when he tortured me? Where was his love when...?!"

"MYST!" Shiva barked, forcing her back. "I said stand down!"

"She stands there, smug as a human, talking about how a sociopath like Luco is capable of love?!" Myst demanded. "How? HOW CAN A MONSTER LIKE HIM LOVE?!"

"Calm down and we'll find out!" Shiva snapped.

Myst hated this whole thing. She hated having to work with humans; she hated that she was being stone-walled by her own pack mate and a glorified pet. Everything about this infuriated her to no end.

But before her anger could blind her, she saw Drake, standing between the wolves and the dragon. Ready to defend Blaze...

The same way Myst felt she was ready to defend the wolves.

Myst forced herself to breath. She needed the dragons on her side if she was going to stop Luco. A part of Myst always wanted the dragons to understand her and to join her in her campaign. And now, she had the chance to show them she was better.

It hurt Myst on another level to wait, but she stood down, and let Shiva's focus turn back to Blaze.

Blaze looked like she was struggling not to laugh. However, her laugh faded with Shiva's next words.

"I understand you."

Blaze paused, as Shiva touched the ground between them. In the memories that formed between Blaze and Shiva, the group saw a cabin in the woods. Shiva, as a regular dog, sitting by the hearth fire, partially in the lap of her old master. The elder human softly stroked Shiva's head, as her eyes were shut in content happiness.

"I understand loving your master," Shiva continued. "I understand wanting to protect him."

Myst wanted to retort that Luco didn't deserve protection. But she didn't dare speak; Blaze's eyes dilated; her expression changed from determined to confused.

"I'm not judging you," Shiva assured the dragon. "All I want is the truth."

Blaze stared at Shiva for what felt like an eternity. Briefly, she looked to Drake, and the General nodded in assurance. Myst narrowed her eyes, waiting for Blaze to try and pull something. But instead...

"He made me," Blaze said. "Made us all to save humanity from themselves."

Myst glowered. "Themselves?"

Blaze nodded at Myst. "You and your wolves are the ones who purge; you rid the world of cruel and evil humans. And we?" Blaze indicated herself. "We rescue the ones that are capable of changing. But just barely; just enough so that they know not to become like the people you kill."

Myst clenched her claws. "What about Luco?" she demanded. "He's just like the people I killed; he tortured me. Tortured my friends!"

"A necessary sacrifice," Blaze replied sadly. "One that had to be done so you would not falter in your duty."

Shiva narrowed her eyes. "So, war and murder are his answers?" she asked, as another image formed between them: the skull of Shiva's master. "My master deserved to die?"

Myst couldn't help but grin as the dragon's determined gaze faltered in the wake of Shiva's tranquil fury.

"Collateral damage," Blaze said. "Unfortunate, but necessary."

Myst glanced at the General. "Is that true, General Drake," she asked. "Is human collateral damage necessary?"

Drake shook his head. "No," he said, looking to Blaze in disappointment. "That's not what you were supposed to be taught."

Blaze shrugged. "That's what he taught me. He is my rider; he is my father. He believes in his reasons for what he does. And he will come for me. That's not defiant talk." She glanced at Myst. "I don't know how he found the resolve to hurt Myst... but I do know that he loves me. He won't leave me here." She sighed. "You should prepare. Your attempts for peace have scared him. He will do his best to turn one more dragon against you – keep you from turning them from their duty - but once that's done, he'll come for me."

Myst narrowed her eyes. "Who is he meeting?"

Blaze grinned. She lowered her head, and an image appeared before her: a large, humanoid dragon, different from Rocket or Blaze, much like Swift and Jackknife had been. However, this new dragon had no wings, feathered or otherwise, and her white scales were solid unlike Jackknife's watery visage. If it weren't for the diamond white scales across her body or her reptilian face and tail, it would be easy to mistake her for a human. Kind of like the human who stood next to her; a mountain of a man with stone-brown skin. His face was mushed like a pug; his black hair shaved almost to nonexistence. A massive axe was strapped to his back, and his rider uniform had a patch depicting a steer. With his large frame, it was hard to tell which one was the human and which one the dragon.

Shiva's ears flattened. She sighed. "I shouldn't even ask, should I?"

"That's Diamondback," Drake said. "And her rider Brock Bronson. They're third only to me and Luco in authority: Diamondback can use her power over earth to rebuild what's destroyed in the fights, so they're in charge of helping the people after we've run through." He turned to Shiva. "By now, they likely would've made a beeline for the last town where Myst and Luco fought; Diamondback will want to make sure it's repaired as soon as possible."

Shiva nodded, and turned back to Blaze. "Thank you."

"You shouldn't thank me," Blaze mused. "Just because I see good in him, doesn't mean he won't give you a fight. Dragons and demi-wolves must fight. Or humanity is doomed to become the very evil we were made to destroy."

With those ominous words, the bridge dissipated, and they found themselves back in the interrogation room.

Shiva was gone, but Blaze still stared at the spot where the white wolf had stood. Blaze's fire died down, and though the ice water still steamed, it no longer boiled with her rage.

Myst and Drake turned as the door opened, and Rocket and Connors walked in.

"Well?"

"Luco's meeting with Diamondback," Myst said. "Luco believes that somehow, the fights between dragons and demi-wolves are keeping humans from committing crimes, and that we're getting in the way of that." She nodded at Rocket. "That's why he tried to turn Swift and Jackknife against you; he wants the dragons to think Rocket's crazy and that we're still evil so we'll keep fighting and scare the humans into being good and safe."

Connors scoffed. "Then he clearly has no idea what safety looks like." He looked to Fawkes, who stood in the door frame. "We'll have to teach him that."

Myst's eyes narrowed. "I'd like to teach him." She flared her claws.

Drake grimaced and even Connors frowned, before the King waved a hand. "That is assuming you have a location?"

Myst nodded. "We do."

"Alright?" Connors said. "You two should head out." He turned to his bodyguard. "Fawkes, you know what to do."

Fawkes saluted, before noticing Drake glaring toward them.

"I'm still not convinced this is a good idea," Drake said. "How do we know you're not going to kill him, especially now?"

"I took a vow," Myst growled. "And unlike humans, wolves honor their promises."

"Did you promise to wipe out every human on the planet?" Drake asked. "What happened to that promise?"

Myst tensed, while Drake gazed sadly at Rocket. "I'm sorry, Rocket, but Swift still thinks something's wrong with you, and he's not alone. People have been coming to me; asking why I'm not locking you up for associating with these wolves. They want me to take action and I can't hold them back much longer."

"But sir, we're close," Rocket insisted, flexing her claws. "You know Myst isn't…"

"Isn't what?" Drake scoffed. "How do I know you're really on board with this whole situation? How do we know Myst isn't messing with your head with that 'pack link' thing?" He shook his head. "I still think it was a mistake to send you out there so soon after Buck's death, and I still think it was wrong-headed to give you a demi-wolf as his replacement. If it was my choice, I'd have you stop this and rest. Make sure you're really fine before we send you back out there." He turned to Connors. "I can send Bang and Dixon after Luco right now."

Connors took out a silver flask and took a long, slow draw from it and then exhaled deliberately. "And how can we trust that Luco won't turn Bang and Dixon against you. Myst knows who Luco really is, and Rocket is the only dragon willing to believe her. There's no other alternative."

Drake looked to Rocket. "Is that true, Rocket? Do you really believe this demi-wolf has somehow changed from the monster we've been fighting all these years?"

Myst growled, but Rocket spread a wing between her and the General. Rocket gazed into Drake's eyes; for so many years, his word had been law in her heart. She had trusted him with her life.

But now, for the first time ever... he was wrong about this.

She didn't want to say it. Her heart hammered in her throat. But with Myst behind her, and all eyes watching her, Rocket forced herself to answer.

"Myst has saved my life twice and gone along with our restrictions," she said. "She is my Rider now, no matter the history between us. We can do this."

Drake frowned, his fiery eyes flashing with fury. He and his dragon glared each other down for one second; two seconds; three. Myst's skin crawled under her fur; she had no idea how Connors was so calm, or where Rocket had pulled this strength of will from.

Finally, Drake sighed. "If this goes sideways...," he warned Rocket, before he let the threat hang in the air, and left the room.

As he left, Myst noticed Rocket shivering. The red dragon let out a low, shaky breath, before she sunk to a sitting position.

"I can't believe I did that," she mumbled.

Myst lightly punched her shoulder. "Thank you."

Rocket didn't even look at her. "I can't believe I just did that."

"Don't beat yourself up," Connors replied. "Drake's a passionate man, but he doesn't tend to think for the long term. Even the greatest of us needs guidance from others sometimes." He glanced at Myst. "Speaking of which… what exactly is your plan?"

Myst looked back at Blaze.

"We're going back to the fishing town," Myst said. "If Drake is right, Diamondback will head over there to fix up the town after our fight. And Luco will be waiting for her."

"What about Jackknife?" Fawkes asked.

Rocket cricked her neck, but when Myst looked to her, she could see the trust she had earned shining in the dragon's eyes.

"I think Jackknife can be convinced," Rocket said. "He already saw how we tried to protect the town, and how Luco tried to have us attack Fawkes."

Myst nodded, turning back to the King. "One way or another, we're coming back with Luco in chains."

Chapter 9: A Wing and a Prayer

Rocket's heart wouldn't stop beating in her throat as she approached the fishing town again. With every beat of her red wings, the duo got closer and closer to Luco. And by extension, that meant Rocket was bringing Myst closer and closer to the man she wanted nothing more than to kill and torture in retaliation for what he did to her. How ironic that she had to prevent Myst from doing the same thing.

Rocket said she trusted Myst. And yet… trust was easier when it was simple. But this relationship was anything but simple.

And speaking of trust, how could Rocket trust Blaze? What if the fire dragon tricked them? What if the pack link missed something? General Drake didn't trust it; why should she? And even if the pack link was legitimate… Blaze said Luco prepped her mind for it. What if he was somehow prepared for them? Jackknife was still back there too, wasn't he? What if Luco somehow turned him again?

"You seem perturbed at Blaze's loyalty," Myst commented from Rocket's back, breaking her out of her cloud of doubts. "Is that a bad thing among Riders?"

Rocket grimaced. "Of course not. But… at the same time, we need to be prepared for loss. We were made to be the guardians of Gaia and the humans who walk her surface. And that's not a job that comes without risk."

"Sure," Myst said. "But, at the same time… Aren't you guys given to Riders after hatching? Shiva's pack link showed us Drake giving you to Buck when you were barely out of the egg." Her ears flattened, and she looked away. "Forgive me for asking, but… what happened… after? Normally?"

"After what?"

Myst didn't reply; she didn't have to. Rocket knew what she was implying, but her new respect for the dragon kept her from putting it into words. For a time, she was silent.

"Forget it," Myst decided. "You don't need to tell me."

Rocket thought about it. "Now's not a good time, and I don't really know how to describe how I feel about it," she decided. "If you want to use the pack link, go ahead."

For a moment, Myst hesitated. But Rocket supposed Shiva or some other demi-wolf's curiosity got the better of them. Because as the pack link spiraled to life, Rocket let her memories speak for her:

A time when a dragon returned home without his rider. Drake was disappointed, but unlike Rocket, the dragon didn't have his killer with him.

Drake patted the dragon's side, and the scene shifted to a new rider. The dragon was grimacing with distrust, but he allowed the new human to mount him. And together, they flew off to wherever they were needed.

Myst tensed. "You just… get a new partner? Just like that? No funeral?"

Rocket scoffed. "Isn't it the same for wolves? You guys lost plenty of pack mates too. And at the end of the day, the roles of the lost still needed to be filled."

"Yeah, but…"

Myst's memories answered this time: a group of demi-wolves, gathered around a mound of the lost. Rocket gaped as, in the memory, *the wolves skinned their former comrades, adding their*

pelts to their armor, and crafting their bones into weapons and
armor.

"You… skin your own kind?" Rocket demanded.

"It ensures that their memory, their presence, stays with us," Myst insisted. She touched her armor, which was interwoven with several patches of fur. "Every wolf that I have lost is with me; whether in my thoughts, or protecting me long after their deaths. While I did have to make sure others could fulfill their roles, none of them were ever expendable."

"It's the same for us," Rocket said. "It's humiliating and demoralizing to lose your rider. I'm not sure what it's like for humans, but I hate the fact that I lost Buck. Not a day goes by where I don't wish…"

"That it could've been different," Myst admitted, still looking at the patches on her armor. "Thinking, 'if I had done something different, they'd still be alive.'"

"You could've done something different," Rocket said. "You could have... well…"

"Let them suffer?" Myst asked. "Let them live in servitude? Not all of the wolves were like Shiva, Rocket. Plenty came from horrendous homes."

Rocket wished she could refute Myst. Unfortunately, Rocket knew the truth: if Luco could exist, there surely had to be others who were just as bad, if not worse. And those poor dogs…

Rocket chuckled hollowly. "Poor dogs?" she asked herself, rubbing her snout. "I really am a disgrace to the dragons."

"Don't think that," Myst said, her eyes darting up as the fishing town came into view. "When we bring Luco back, you'll be a hero. Not just to the humans or dragons… but to the demi-wolves as well. But in order to be that hero, you gotta stay focused, and bring Luco down."

Rocket's grimace faded. Despite everything, she couldn't help but feel a sense of pride in being a hero. Even for demi-wolves.

And with Myst's words encouraging her, she focused on the fishing town, and spotted Diamondback.

It was hard to miss the dragon; Blaze's memories did a bad job capturing the diamond-like sheen of her scales, twinkling and sparkling in the sunlight like the dragon was made of the gems. She was making her way through the fishing village, her lapis-blue eyes were narrow in annoyance. Though Diamondback appeared to be doing nothing but sweeping her hands around like she was brushing away imaginary dirt, the village was in constant motion; burn marks faded from scorched homes, wrecked stalls rebuilt themselves in seconds. Wherever Diamondback stepped, the destruction faded. The citizens stood near Jackknife, who was looking over the many people watching Diamondback as she worked. All either let Jackknife check them over, tended to each other's injuries, or just smiled as Diamondback repaired their homes.

But there were two humans separate from the group of people who followed Diamondback; Luco and what had to be Brock. As Rocket glided back into town, his hazel eyes alighted on her like she was just what he hoped for.

"Look," Luco said. "You see what I mean? A dragon working with the demi-wolves!"

Rocket narrowed her eyes. Myst's fur glowed as Shiva said something Rocket couldn't hear to the dark demi-wolf.

"It'll be okay, Shiva," Myst assured her. "Diamondback and dragons like her never liked fighting; just building. We can handle one more dragon being angry with us."

Let's hope, Rocket's thoughts murmured, before she landed before Diamondback, Brock and Luco with a grin.

"Hey DB," Rocket greeted. "What's up?"

Diamondback raised an eyebrow, though her lapis-blue eyes didn't shine with suspicion like Jackknife's did. "The sky," she replied, before peering at Myst. "Luco was just telling me about this interesting partnership of yours."

"Correction," Brock said, in a low, rumbling voice. "He was telling *me.* You, Diamondback, were working on fixing this town."

Diamondback scoffed, before turning back to her repairs.

Rocket chuckled, while Myst glared at Luco.

"It's over, Luco," Myst said. "You don't have Blaze to save you this time."

Luco just laughed. But Rocket noticed an edge to his laugh; like he was trying to make up for something. Fear, perhaps. "Save me? So, what do you intend to do? Kill me like all the other humans?" He looked to Diamondback. "Diamondback, I know you're not…"

"You talk," Brock rumbled. "To me." He stepped between Luco and Diamondback, barely glancing back at his dragon. "Diamondback, finish your work. I'll handle these guys."

Diamondback growled. "I can multi-task," she insisted. "You don't seriously expect me to just sit on the sidelines and let them harm a fellow rider, do you?"

"I expect you to wait and watch before acting," Brock replied, before turning his dark eyes to Rocket. "Now, Ignis-Drake R065; you know the rules about fighting humans…" He glared at Myst. "And wolves."

Diamondback pointed at Myst. "I just cleaned this place up, I'll have you know; I don't need you wrecking it again!"

Rocket winced, before a fabulous idea sprouted in her mind.

"We're not murderers," Rocket replied, turning to Luco. "In fact, Blaze is still alive right now. Don't you want to see her? After all the loyalty she's shown you, it's the least you can do for her."

Brock blinked, before turning to Luco. "A fair point, Luco. There's no good reason why you should be abandoning your dragon."

Luco whistled, though the edge in his voice grew sharper. "Funny," he mused. "You let Rocky here lecture me about loyalty when she abandoned Buck."

As Rocket struggled to contain her flames, Luco tried to turn to Diamondback, who was listening curiously as she worked. However, Brock stepped between them with a look that discouraged Luco from trying to talk to her.

"Can you believe this dragon?" Luco insisted to Brock as he indicated Rocket. "She loses her own rider to these creatures, and yet now she wants to be friends with them?"

Diamondback hummed, but turned back to her work before Brock could glare at her.

"A… fair point," Brock admitted reluctantly, before turning to Rocket. "Why work with these beasts?"

"We aren't beasts," Myst growled. "We're living creatures that are tired of being abused and…"

"…and discriminated against," Diamondback drawled with a roll of her eyes. "Blah-blah-blah-blah, we've heard it all before."

"And they're trying to change," Rocket added quickly. "Means you wouldn't have to rebuild so much, Diamondback."

Diamondback hummed, intrigued. "Oh?"

"Diamondback…" Brock warned.

"Listen to your rider…" Luco tried to say, but Rocket spoke over him.

"Think about it," she insisted. "Without dragons and demi-wolves fighting, everything you fix wouldn't constantly be broken. You'd be able to work more with Drake, helping him command the dragons."

Myst blinked. *"Is that true?"* she whispered.

Rocket merely grinned as Diamondback mulled it over, looking legitimately interested.

"Terra-Drake 0184," Brock barked.

"They're fooling you…" Luco tried to say, before Diamondback cut him off with a growl of frustration.

"I'm trying to work on this town, Brock!" she snarled at her rider. "It's not my fault they're the ones walking in here and wasting my time!" She glared at Rocket and Myst. "Don't you realize how exhausting this is to do day after day?"

Myst's fur glowed, and Myst chuckled. "Shiva's right; you technically just walked around and waved your arms."

"Myst!" Rocket hissed, but Diamondback just scoffed.

"Of course, a beast like you might interpret it that way," she grumbled, before sweeping away from them. "Alright fine, Rider Brock. Since you're so convinced I'm going to let this village get destroyed again…"

Before Luco could protest, Diamondback swept her tail with a flourish, and the entire villa – people and buildings alike – suddenly lifted up on an entire plate of earth. Diamondback lifted the plate like she was a waiter serving a very large tray of food, and sauntered off.

Brock sighed. "Thank you, DB," he said, before lumbering after her. Meanwhile the people – and Jackknife - rushed to keep up with their rapidly moving homes.

"Think about it, DB," Rocket barked after her. "You won't have to rebuild so much if Luco's brought to justice!"

But with Brock behind her, Diamondback didn't deign to even turn around and acknowledge the sentiment. And in only a few moments, Luco, Rocket and Myst were left on a grassy clearing next to the river, the village a safe distance away. Diamondback shot a look at Jackknife, and the water dragon quickly ran to the edge of town, glaring at the three like a bodyguard as he and Brock planted themselves as sentinels at the town's entrance.

Somehow, Rocket noticed, Brock managed to look more intimidating than Jackknife. Though that could be due to Bai Long being visible in Jackknife's water armor, constantly glancing at Brock and trying to replicate his stance. Jackknife groaned in displeasure at his rider's antics. Meanwhile, Diamondback continued her work, her back turned on the three.

Luco blinked in disbelief, before Rocket got an idea.

"You know," the dragon whispered. "I hate to admit it, but you were right. It took a while to beat any loyalty to you out of Blaze, but when she finally snapped?" Rocket grinned at the fire of outrage glowing in Luco's eyes, even as he tried to hide it behind his smirk. "Worth every moment."

Luco struggled to keep his smile up. "Nice try," he growled. "But I know you, Rocket. You're soft, and Blaze is stronger than you. Nothing you could do would ever turn her on me." He started to walk after Diamondback. "Just like how nothing you do will stop me from getting the dragons to see you as the mad-lizard you are."

"You'd be surprised," Myst noted, her golden eyes sparkling with – hopefully fake – malice. "After all, we wolves have a few tricks up our sleeves." She gave a mocking bow. "Thank you for being such an inspiring teacher. I made sure Blaze knew exactly where I learned my techniques from."

Luco shivered, though it didn't seem to be from the cold. "Okay, girls, this joke's getting a little old, and I've got other things to do…" he started to say.

"Oh, what's the matter?" Rocket asked. "You didn't seem to find the joke bad when you did it to me. Well, that's just what we did. I'm sure Myst got quite the kick out of hearing Blaze's squeal when I…"

Rocket paused, wondering what she could possibly say to provoke Luco enough. Lying did not come easily to her, but she had to provoke him enough to attack – just as he had done to her.

But it turned out she didn't need to provoke him further. Turning back, he pulled out his baseball bat in one hand, and held up his other. Red light crackled to life across his palm, and a strange rune materialized across his skin.

"You've messed with the wrong Rider," he said, before he moved.

Faster than Rocket could blink, he closed the gap between them, striking her with force far beyond a normal human.

"Rocket!" Myst yelped, jumping from Rocket to seize Luco as Rocket staggered, clutching her throbbing head.

Pack link tendrils coursed out of Myst as Shiva tried to snag Luco, only for an explosion like fireworks to throw Myst into Rocket, nearly sending both dragon and demi-wolf tumbling into the water. Meanwhile, the pack link went dark.

"Shiva?" Myst stammered, pawing at her fur. "Shiva! Respond!"

Luco's laugh rang long and loud. "Ladies, if the pack link worked so well on Blaze, why didn't you think about the preparations I had in mind for myself?" He turned to Jackknife and Bai Long, who were being held back by an irritated looking Brock.

"Never fear, you three. I've defended myself against the brainwashing power of Shiva!"

"Wait, what?!" Jackknife stammered.

"What brainwashing power?" Bai Long asked.

Brock sighed, rubbing his temples like he had a headache. "One more problem to deal with…"

"Get up, Myst," Rocket hissed, pulling herself up. "Get up! If he gets away again…"

"That's not gonna happen," Myst snarled, baring her claws as she jumped off Rocket and lunged at Luco again. "I don't need Shiva to rip your face apart!"

But Luco cackled and spun wildly with his bat, meeting Myst's charge. His bat crashed across her claws, and fireworks exploded once more.

Brock started to let Jackknife approach but Luco… waved him off?

"Tend to Rocket!" Luco said. "Help her free herself of this madness!" He dodged Myst's strikes. "I got this she-dog!"

Myst valiantly held her ground, and the two dueled along the shoreline. They punched, kicked, grappled and bit. Luco seized

Myst's mane and yanked it down, but Myst ripped her head free of the mane and mask and continued, her scars on full display as she tried to add cuts to Luco's face.

Jackknife and his rider tensed with worry, before Bai Long drove his dragon towards Rocket.

"Rocket, what's he talking about?" Bai Long demanded.

"I was right, wasn't I?" Jackknife noted. "You were brainwashed?"

"What, no!" Rocket protested.

But as the battle before them continued, Rocket realized Luco was falling back. With her vision still blurred, she couldn't tell if he was smirking in victory, or his scar was just distorting his grin more than usual. Myst, however, was flying into a frenzy; hacking, spitting and roaring as she drove Luco back. Her golden eyes were shining with a mad light, and her teeth bared in a demonic smile as she kept forcing Luco further and further back.

Jackknife was watching the whole thing with trepidation. Back in the village, Diamondback's attention was pulled from her work.

"Brock?" she asked.

"It's alright, DB," Brock said. "You stay with that village; don't you worry about nothing."

Diamondback growled in dissatisfaction, and Brock looked to Rocket, as if expecting her to do something.

"That's it!" Rocket realized.

Before Jackknife could get up, Rocket grabbed his talon.

"Jackknife, wait," she said. "Let me prove I'm not brainwashed."

Jackknife glanced at Luco. "Is it gonna involve him dying?"

"I won't let him die," Rocket argued. "No matter what, we don't kill humans. That's what Drake taught us."

Jackknife grimaced, but didn't refute her. Bai Long, however, grinned, and stepped back.

"What do you think, Jack," he said. "If she's not here to kill him… it's hard to believe she's brainwashed."

"Maybe," Jackknife grumbled, glaring at her. "But I still don't like you fire dragons." Rocket sighed. "We're on the same side, Jackknife," she insisted. "And I'll prove it." She stepped past her watery counterpart just as Myst cut Luco's bat in half with a brutal slash. The crazed rider's back hit the sand, and Myst seized him by the neck, drawing her claw up to slice his face.

"STOP!" Rocket roared. For a second, her fire glowed at the back of her throat.

But, much to her relief, Myst obeyed. Rocket didn't see a pack link constraining her, but Myst's claws hovered in the air. Her gums glowed pink against her white teeth, and her eyes were locked on Luco's with hatred. But still, she froze.

"Come on," Luco hissed. "What're you waiting for? This is your moment, isn't it? The part where you finally take revenge?"

"What're you talking about?" Jackknife demanded. "Rocket, get 'er away from him."

"Don't worry Jack," Rocket insisted, keeping her eyes on Myst. "Myst, I understand what you've been trying to tell me; people like Luco are scum, and... maybe they don't deserve life."

"WHAT?!" Bai Long, Jackknife and even Brock boomed.

Myst tore her eyes from Luco, fixing on Rocket with disbelief.

"But when we adopt their methods," Rocket continued. "We become the very evil we mean to destroy."

"Yawn," Luco drawled sarcastically. "If you're so concerned about me, Rocket, how about you save me with a fireball or something?"

Rocket glowered. "No," she said, looking to Myst. "Myst is my rider. And I trust her to do what's right."

Myst blinked in shock at Rocket's words. She slowly lowered her claw, looking at them in thought. Luco rolled his eyes.

"You're really gonna listen to her?" Luco whispered at Myst. "Your biggest obstacle. Now's the perfect time, Misty; you've got me at your mercy. After everything I've done... why should you listen to a word that dragon says?"

Myst glared at him, but the rage in her eyes faded to cold indifference.

"Because I made a vow," she said, before releasing him. "And your fate is in Connors hands."

She looked to Rocket, and the dragon nodded with a grin. Behind her, Jackknife started to relax, exchanging a surprised look with Bai Long. Even Brock's stoic façade cracked in surprise, sharing a stunned look with Diamondback. But then...

"How sweet," Luco mocked. "For me." He threw something at Rocket, Bai Long and Jackknife's feet. Smoke billowed up, blinding the dragons just as she heard Myst cry out in pain.

Rocket didn't think. The oxygen ignited in her throat; the fireball shot from her maw.

BOOM!

The smoke cleared. Myst stood in front of Rocket. Still alive. Still okay.

Even better, the pack link spiraled back to life, tendrils wrapping around Rocket's talons when she reached out for them.

"I'm here! Wait, I'm here!" Shiva's voice barked out of Myst. *"Myst don't..."* she paused. *"Uh... what happened?"*

Myst and Rocket said nothing, as all eyes fell on Luco. The grass sizzled around his downed form, showing Rocket the extent of the damage.

The man's skin was blackened and charred, and he lay limp. A low moan of pain wheezed out of his cracked lips.

Diamondback's voice came back, trembling in shock. "Rocket... w-what did you do?"

Rocket's breath caught in her throat. She looked back as Li and Jackknife stepped away from her, their eyes wide in betrayal. Brock had his axe out, looking ready to strike if she stepped towards Diamondback and the town.

Instantly, Rocket realized how bad this all looked; The pack link connecting her and Myst, Luco charred and blackened like an overcooked piece of beef.

"Jackknife, please, it's not what you think!" Rocket insisted, looking to Brock. "Brock…"

But Jackknife and Bai Long spun and dove into the river, vanishing with barely a splash. When Rocket looked to Diamondback, Brock stepped closer.

"You stay away from this town and my dragon," he growled, his voice somehow deeper and scarier than before.

Rocket could only shake her head. She had burned a human. She had hit him with her fire, and…

A memory shot into her mind: Drake standing over her.

"To use your fire against man is the greatest crime a dragon can commit," he warned. "Any dragon that would see humans die like wolves is no better than the wolves themselves."

Rocket felt her blood chill at the conditioned memory. It didn't help when Myst's voice sounded.

"Rocket?" she asked. "Rocket, take it easy. You saved my life."

Rocket's teeth bared. "He started this whole war," Rocket snarled at Diamondback and Brock. "He deserved this!"

"I know," Myst assured her. "Believe me, I know…"

Rocket whirled on Myst. "You stay out of this," Rocket insisted. "I only did this to protect the people. He… they're safe now. He can't hurt them!"

Yet, despite her words, she couldn't get rid of the chill running through her entire body. And evidently, neither could Diamondback or Brock, who watched Rocket like she had truly gone insane.

"*We can heal him,*" Shiva offered through Myst.

Myst blinked. "Now?"

"*Of course not,*" Shiva barked indignantly. "*I may be compassionate, but I'm not crazy.*"

"Take him back to the humans," Luke's voice offered. *"But be careful; I've seen this guy fight before; he got beat way too easily for my liking. Something else is going on here."*

"Well, we won't know his motivations if he dies," Shiva noted.

Reluctantly nodding in agreement, Rocket crept closer to Luco, who gazed at her with pain-ridden fear.

"Supposed... to take me alive..." he moaned.

Rocket growled, wishing she could fry the doubt and despair in her gut. *Why do I have to feel bad about this?* Rocket wanted to scream. *After all the grief, pain and drama he caused?*

She snatched him up, grimacing when he let out a scream of agony. "Lucas Cooper," she growled. "You're under arrest."

He smacked cracked lips. "Think I'll... live long enough?" he wheezed.

Myst stepped up, winding a pack link around his wrist. "You'll live," she said. "Long enough for Connors to pass judgement."

Luco didn't even have the strength to chuckle. Rocket seethed as Myst draped the downed human across her back. This was supposed to be a good thing: she had gotten the bad guy. Peace was going to be achieved! She had won!

Yet, as his cracked and sizzling body settled over her scales, and Diamondback and Brock glared at Rocket when she looked at them, a heavy weight dropped from what should have been victory into doubt and horror.

Yelling at humans – even disagreeing with her General – was one thing. But she assaulted a human! She had used her fire on the very species she was sworn to protect.

"B-But I had to!" she tried to justify in her mind. *"He was bad."*

But her heart refused to agree.

Chapter 10: The Right Thing?

Myst expected Luco's defeat to be more… triumphant.

She expected that – if she wasn't allowed to dispose of Luco properly – that they would return to the Walls of Cadmus, with Luco in chains and the humans in shock that a dragon and a demi-wolf managed to work together for his capture. The King would give that nod of respect he gave Shiva, and people would start to think, '*Hey, that demi-wolf's not so bad. Maybe we were wrong to be so cruel to them, even before they evolved. Maybe we should change.*'

Instead, the humans watched as Myst and Rocket carried Luco's charred body into the city. And Myst didn't need the pack link to see that what they were thinking was the exact opposite of what she hoped for.

"Teeth-For-Days' Fangs," Drake muttered as Rocket brought in Luco. "R-Rocket… what did…?"

"He should be grateful we let him live," Myst growled. "He attacked us."

Drake glared at Myst, but didn't reply. Connors motioned to his bodyguard Fawkes, who gave him a worried look. However, when he motioned again, she reluctantly stepped forward, and took Luco from Rocket's talons.

"You better put him in a cell," was what Myst wanted to say. But as she opened her mouth, Shiva's voice came out instead. *"We stabilized him during the flight here, and we have the power to heal him. Under your direction, of course."*

But Drake shook his head. "You've done quite enough for now," he said.

Connors looked like he had something he wanted to say, but instead… "Fawkes, get the medics."

Fawkes nodded, and left.

A long and uncomfortable silence occurred while waiting for the medics.

Myst glanced between the stoic humans and her nervous dragon. "We have the power to heal him now," she noted.

"General," Rocket said. "He gave us no choice."

Silence was Drake's only answer.

It was a relief when the medics finally arrived. Strapping Luco down onto a gurney, they raced him into the city, with the three humans beside him. Just before they left, however, Connors looked back.

"Thank you both," he said, his tone formal. Then he walked back into his city, the guards shutting the gates.

Myst's ears flattened. "Can you believe this, Rocket?" she demanded.

But when she looked to Rocket, she found the dragon's eyes downcast. Rocket turned and began to walk away.

"Wait a minute," Myst protested, following Rocket. "Didn't we just win? Luco's defeated, peace has been protected, and you and I were able to work together! All things considered, this should be a great day!"

For a moment, Rocket was silent, gazing out at the forests beyond the field.

"You know," Rocket mused. "I spent so much time in those forests, hunting you guys, trying to defend humans that wandered in there. And yet... I never took the time to take it all in. Smell the pine... watch the leaves change color..." She lowered her head.

"What are you talking about?" Myst asked. "We did the right thing."

Rocket looked at Myst, her eyes steaming with tears. "Then why does it feel so wrong? I committed sacrilege, Myst; I burned a human."

"A human that forced us to fight in an endless, pointless war," Myst countered.

Rocket sighed, shaking her head. "You can't possibly understand, can you?" she growled.

Myst's brow furrowed, and she cautiously touched the dragon's shoulder. Letting the pack link flow, she offered up a memory to Rocket: *a wolf climbing to his paws, freshly mutated into a demi-wolf. Myst leading him to a village.*

"I understand more than you know," Myst whispered. "When I evolved my pack mates, many were confused. Not all of their owners made their abuse blatant..." She grimaced. "And... 'maybe'... not all of them were abusive to begin with. Either way... I had to convince them. If you hadn't intervened, I would have done this for Shiva as well."

The memory showed Myst taking the new demi-wolf to the outskirts of town. There, she showed him how several older boys were shoving a woman into the shadows. The woman was terrified, and the boys were smiling. Practically reveling in her fear. At least, until they saw the wolves coming for them.

Rocket seethed, before the fire left her eyes. She hung her head. "Humanity... all I've ever wanted to do was defend it. See the good that it could do. Be the catalyst to protect them so that the good they are capable of could be done."

Myst pursed her lips. "I... can't believe I'm saying this, but... maybe there is still good in them, in many of them."

Rocket nodded, a memory showing *Buck confidently steering her through the air. Making her land between a group of wolves and a fleeing human. Smiling confidently at the human.*

"This is no place for a lady like yourself," he said to her. "Go! We got this!"

And he didn't just sit on Rocket's back and direct her; Buck got off and fought alongside his dragon. Rocket smiled at the memory.

"He was a good man," Rocket said, her smile fading as she looked back at the forest. "I just... wish everyone else was as good."

Myst's ears flattened. "You're not the only one."

Rocket glanced at Myst, before chuckling. For a moment, they just peered into the forest together, taking it all in.

Myst felt her tail wag unconsciously. A small part of her always held out hope for the dragons; a small belief that maybe, just maybe, they would come to know the truth. And yet Myst also knew that Rocket would never fully see humans the way she did. She didn't have the same experiences or the same conditioning.

But is that really a bad thing? She couldn't help but ponder.

"You've been a good rider, Myst." Rocket noted, tearing Myst out of her thoughts. "But..." Her grin faded. "Now that Luco's been... well, what will you do?"

Myst hummed, glancing at the forest. "Well, I have my pack waiting for me," she noted half-heartedly. "Kodo's going to be happy to see me, at least." Her grin faded as she looked up at Rocket. "But what about you? What will you do?"

Rocket gripped her wings. "Technically, I'm supposed to go back and wait for Drake to assign me a new Rider. But... well, everyone already seems to think that you're my new rider... so..."

She glanced at Myst again, and Myst straightened in shock.

"You want me... to stay your rider?" Myst asked.

"Yeah, I know, it's stupid," Rocket said quickly, looking away. "I shouldn't have brought it up, it's…"

"No-no!" Myst stammered. "I…"

Myst paused; what could she say to that? She always wanted a dragon to be on her side; every time she saw them flying through the air, humans on their backs, she couldn't help but see them as pets; slaves that had to be freed.

But Myst knew Rocket wasn't a slave to be freed; she understood Rocket was a dragon with her own thoughts and opinions. And those opinions included a belief in humans, no matter what Luco or any other tyrant did to dissuade her.

Before Myst could respond, Rocket looked toward the forest. "Oh, what's that?" she noted. "I'm-a go check it out."

"But, Rocket…" Myst tried to say.

But Rocket blasted off with a burst of fire and was gone before Myst could say another word.

Myst couldn't help but notice that Rocket left her with the humans.

She must really trust me, Myst realized. Smiling at the thought, Myst decided to honor that trust. Putting her back to the city, she made for home. Back to the wolves; back to Kodo.

And yet… something still tugged on the back of her mind. Luco's evil laugh. His cruel hands, throwing her in a world of rage and pain. Rocket's despair at what she did to him, combined with the frosty reception their return had gotten.

What exactly was going to be Luco's punishment?

As Myst turned back, however, she felt Shiva's pack link surging through her.

"Myst, I know what you're thinking," Shiva warned. *"Don't do it."*

"I just want to make sure, Shiva," Myst promised. "I'm not going to hurt anyone."

"The people don't know that," Shiva insisted. *"Now come home. Job's done; we're fine now."*

"We miss you, Myst," Kodo's voice added. *"Please come back."*

His voice should have convinced Myst. Getting to see that silver wolf's eyes light up with joy… it should have been enough.

Yet Myst's gut wasn't satisfied. *"After everything he did to us, can we really trust Connors to follow through?"*

The others were silent, but Myst could feel Luke's anger brimming through the link. He knew firsthand what Luco had done. Even Shiva wasn't immune; Myst could feel her own tranquil fury at her own encounter with Luco before the arena. When he laughed at her after she saw into his mind.

Even so, Shiva stamped her anger down. *"If Luco finds you worrying about him, it will only inflate his sense of self-righteousness. He's nothing more than a pimple on a gnat's wing. We should treat him as such."*

Luke paused. *"Uh... how can gnats get pimples on their wings?"*

Shiva paused. *"I... dunno. I just remembered my master saying something similar."*

As Shiva and Luke talked, however, Myst instinctually turned back to the city.

"Myst," Celine's voice piped up. *"Don't! If they see you..."*

"*They won't see me, dear Celine,*" Myst assured the young wolf. "*I'll just make sure Luco gets what he deserves, and then I'll leave. No one will know I was there.*"

Her voice caught Shiva's attention, but the white demi-wolf thankfully didn't protest. "*You promise?*"

Myst smiled. "I promise."

Shiva sighed. "*In and out. No one can know.*"

"*Of course.*"

"*And... don't be disappointed. There's probably not going to be a way for them to punish him the way you want them to.*"

Myst sighed. "As long as he's not a threat to you guys, I'll be satisfied."

She could feel Luke and Kodo's hearts swell with joy. "*I told you, Shiva,*" Luke said. "*I told you there was more to her.*"

"*Yes-yes,*" Shiva grumbled. "*You were right and I was wrong.*"

As their voices went quiet, Myst followed Luco's scent. However, two guards stood in her way.

Acting fast, Myst turned right back around and walked until she was out of their sight. Then, turning around, she skirted in a wide arc back towards the city walls.

"Luke," Myst noted. *"You went through here before, right?"*

"Yeah," he said. *"There's a pathway I used to rescue Shiva. Just be careful, though, it's got a couple of guards I had to bulldoze past to get in."*

Shiva grumbled as the pack link hummed. *"I really don't like this,"* she said. *"I know I'm helping, but I reserve my right to grumble about it."*

"Grumble all you want," Myst growled. "Just make sure the guards don't see me." Shiva growled, but as Myst took Luke's path, Shiva's link shot out, quickly snagging any guards Myst encountered, and putting them to sleep, keeping them standing as Myst slunk by, before awakening them and drawing away before the guards knew what hit them.

Past the gates and through the shadows Myst went; avoiding the gazes of humans and shutting off the protests of her heart, demanding these humans be punished.

Punished for what? Her head managed to reply. *It's as Rocket said, 'not all of these humans are bad. We only need to worry about one right now.'*

Myst sensed Shiva smiling. *"I can't believe I'm saying this, but I'm proud of you Myst."*

"Yeah-yeah, I'm as soft as you now," Myst thought with a roll of her eyes. *"Maybe then one of the males will get over being intimidated by me and be my mate, right?"*

Luke barked a laugh. *"Soft females have some advantages,"* he admitted.

Myst grinned, though her grin faded as she followed Luco's scent to a hospital. She noticed a new scent entwining with Luco's. Several new scents, in fact.

"Are those… dragons?" Myst whispered.

"Can't be," Shiva said. *"Unless… is Drake among them?"*

Myst shook her head. *"I'm not getting his scent."* Her ears perked. *"Wait…"* she sniffed closer. *"Sea… feathers…"* She looked up with a gasp. *"That's Swift and Jackknife; the dragons Luco tried to turn against us."*

Myst felt Shiva's blood run cold. *"Oh, no…"*

With paranoia and a need for closure driving her, Myst snuck around the hospital, narrowing Luco's scent down. Thankfully, he was situated on the first floor. But right as she turned the corner, she saw them.

Swift was helping Tex get Luco out of the window and onto his back.

"Steady, Swift," Tex said as she got Luco onto his back. "Steady…"

However, the bird dragon looked up, spotting Myst, and squawked, backing up.

"Swift, dog…" Tex paused, seeing Myst. Immediately, she pulled her firearm, but Myst felt Shiva come to the rescue, her pack link curling out of Myst's body and smacking the firearm into the dirt.

"Don't try it," Shiva growled out of Myst's voice. *"You have five seconds to explain what you're doing."*

"A-Allison…" Swift whimpered, backing up.

"It's okay, Swift," Tex – Allison? – replied, raising her arms in a protective stance as she kept herself between the wolf and dragon. "It's all gonna be fine. Myst has turned over a new leaf. Ain't that right?"

Myst growled. "That won't stop me from killing you if you're doing what I think you're doing."

Tex hummed, backing up further as Myst bore down on her. "Figured as much," she admitted. "Luco was right about you; all you became was more cunning. Orchestrating a whole plan to let the wolves take over, right?"

"That's not what we're doing here," Shiva tried to insist.

Tex smirked. "But not cunning enough though. Luco knew you'd come. And now that Rocket ain't around to protect you..."

Myst narrowed her eyes, and tried to approach. But as she passed the window to Luco's hospital room... she heard a familiar hissing noise.

"It's time to put a stop to dis madness."

Myst spun just as webbed talons closed over her face.

Rocket was weary of surprises. It was bad enough that the humans she was created to protect – some of them, anyway – turned out to be evil. It was another thing that the demi-wolves - which up until recently were her sworn enemy - were actually capable of being something more than savage beasts. But now, fate seemed keen to continue the thinning of the ice of her beliefs, fracturing under every step.

Though she previously escaped from Myst, she could not escape from the cycle of thoughts tormenting her. As she flew over the city, looking for Drake or someone who reminded her of a time when she could fully trust human integrity, she noticed Blaze perched on top of the hospital.

What the… why is she out? Rocket paused as she realized the answer: *Drake. He must have let her go the second we had Luco. At least dragons can't do wrong; we just obey our riders.*

With her thoughts comforting her, Rocket deposited herself next to Blaze.

"Hey Blaze," Rocket greeted.

Blaze gave a small wave.

"Out already? So, I guess no hard feelings about what happened with Luco, right?"

"Mm," Blaze nodded.

Rocket sat next to Blaze. "I'm... sorry either way," she noted. "It's one thing to lose a Rider... it can't be easy to know that your rider was abusing his power."

"Mm."

"Just know that..."

A SLAM startled both dragons. They looked down as a scream sounded from below.

As the scream pierced Rocket's ear drums, Rocket's instinct took over. As one, the two dragons dove off the roof, banking in the air and surging through the window into the room from which the scream came.

But it was too late. Rocket's heart churned at what was inside. The walls were painted with a wet coat of red. A hunk of what looked like raw meat sat on a soaked hospital bed. And right next to it...

"Myst?!" Rocket stammered. "WHAT THE HELL?!"

Myst spun back around, her dark fur coated in red. "Rocket, wait a minute!"

But Rocket had no time for words – and neither did Blaze. As the two dragons launched their fireballs, Myst barely matched them with Shiva's pack link. Their attacks exploded into smoke, and when Blaze fanned the concealing fog away, they saw Myst make a run for it, jumping for the door.

"No you don't!" Rocket snarled, catching Myst by the tail. "You traitorous..."

"Not me!" Myst insisted. "Jackknife! The other dragons! They did this!"

"LIES!" Blaze roared, fire exploding from her. Rocket was forced to release Myst as the room went up in flames.

"IT'S TRUE!" Myst insisted. "They took Luco! We have to stop..."

Blaze cut her off with another kick, but Myst rolled with her fall, lashing out with a pack link that caught Rocket around the neck.

"Please, Rocket," Shiva said. *"At much as I hate to admit it, Myst isn't lying."*

A brief image flashed before Rocket's eyes. *Jackknife seizing Myst by her face. Pulling her into the room. A room that Jackknife had spray painted red. Filled Luco's bed up with raw beef and meat.*

But then the vision cut off, Blaze cutting a talon through the link like she was slicing through spider webs.

"Luco's tricking you!" Myst said. "He…"

But then Blaze hit her with a tail lash, and the dark wolf went down hard. Blaze seized Myst by the nape, looking ready to crush her head.

"Wait!" Rocket yelled.

Blaze whirled on Rocket, her expression eerily familiar. Rocket was aware of that same expression, it was the one she flashed at Shiva when Buck was killed. Even if nothing about this felt right, there was no way she could tell Blaze she was wrong to feel that way.

So, she defaulted to the same reason she used when she previously petitioned Shiva to release her guilt about Buck.

"We're better than them," Rocket insisted. "We need to take her to Drake."

Blaze snorted, no doubt remembering how Drake interrogated her.

"If you kill her right now, you prove you are no better than her," Rocket insisted. "We're supposed to be dragons, Blaze; Drake raised us to be better than that!"

Blaze narrowed her eyes, but lowered her head, unable to disagree with Rocket. At that moment, a voice outside drew their gaze.

"Rocket! Blaze!" Drake's voice boomed. "What is the meaning of this fire! Where is Luco?"

Exchanging a glance, Rocket and Blaze returned outside, Blaze still holding Myst, who hadn't fully recovered consciousness.

Yet, even as they approached the General, doubts burned with Rocket's fire.

Something's up. Swift and Jackknife swallowed Luco's bull before, didn't they? Myst was getting better. So why would she suddenly attack him unless they were making some sort of move?

Rocket noticed Myst waking up. Her golden eyes fluttered open, and she shifted in Blaze's grip looking to Rocket with confusion.

At the same time, Drake stormed up to them. "Rocket!" he barked. "What happened?"

Rocket could only shake her head at Myst. *I'm so sorry, Myst,* she wished she could say. *I wish I could tell what was happening!*

Blaze shook Myst at Drake with a heart-stricken roar. Drake stared at the dark wolf, his disbelief slowly giving way to rage.

"Rocket," he growled. "What did she do?"

"General…" Rocket tried to say. But with everyone's eyes on her, and the circumstantial evidence behind her, Rocket couldn't find the words to defend Myst. "We… 'think' she killed Luco."

"I was set up!" Myst murmured, her head spinning. "Luco…" Her words were cut off as Blaze tightened her grip, strangling Myst.

"Blaze!" Rocket protested. "What about Shiva? This doesn't make…"

"Shiva…" Drake growled. "I knew we couldn't trust a demi-wolf."

Rocket wished she could sew her mouth shut.

Drake nodded to Blaze. "Blaze, give me the wolf."

Reluctantly, Blaze handed Myst over to Drake. Drake handed Myst over to the guards standing with him, who promptly cuffed and muzzled her.

"I'm through screwing around with these dogs," Drake growled. "We have a so-called 'Alpha' to confront."

However, as Drake turned to march Myst to the dungeons, Blaze suddenly turned and flew away. Rocket paused, watching as the yellow dragon.

"Um... Blaze?" Rocket called out. "Where are you going?"

"Leave her," Drake insisted. "She just lost her rider. Give her some space."

But Rocket's eyes narrowed. Blaze was Luco's dragon. What were the odds she was in on this whole thing?

"I'll go check on her," Rocket offered, though her gaze drifted to Myst. "Just call if you need me."

Myst caught her eye, and Rocket gave her a grim nod. She may not have had the pack link, but she thought with all her might, *'Don't lose hope, Myst. I know something's up. I won't let Luco get away with this.'*

Thankfully, Myst seemed to recognize her thoughts. Her own eyes narrowed, and she nodded back, before Drake forced her to march away. Rocket, meanwhile, took off after Blaze, even as the yellow dragon tried her best to become a dot on the horizon.

"Oh, no you don't," Rocket thought darkly. *"You're not getting away from me that easily."*

However, as she found out, she didn't need to go far. No sooner had she taken off after Blaze than the yellow dragon dipped down into the forest just beyond the city. Acting fast, Rocket tucked her wings and dove, following Blaze down toward a creek. A creek where Swift, Tex and – Rocket's heart dropped – Diamondback and Brock were watching Bai Long and Jackknife tend to a burned Luco.

"Come on, Jack," Bai Long insisted. "You're a water dragon; this should be second nature to you."

"It ain't second nature to fire dragons," Jackknife snapped, rubbing water like lotion over Luco's burns. "I ain't gonna be sidelined as some second-hand medic!"

"Well, a medic is what we need right now," Bai Long insisted.

"I still don't understand," Diamondback admitted. "Myst is… still evil?"

"Either that or Rocket's evil," Brock growled. "I still can't believe it; Luco was running for me, and Rocket shot him right in the back."

"Myst was always evil," Bai Long said. "I guess Rocket just turned evil with her."

"No doubt, brother," Jackknife agreed as he struggled to work on Luco. "Lookit dese burns. I'm surprised he's still breathing after dis."

"He'd be breathing easier if you knew what you were doing," Bai Long grumbled.

Jackknife hissed at him before bending closer over Luco.

"B-But what about the General?" Swift asked. "He said she was okay. D-Does that mean the General's evil?"

"Maybe he don't know," Tex replied. "Man ain't a god, after all."

"Nope," Luco mumbled, rising up. "No, he is not."

Rocket slowed, her eyes widening. Jackknife's skills as a healer were far from perfect – it didn't help that he took no pride in them due to seeing them as weak compared to fire powers. But it still hurt to see Luco's skin such an angry shade of red.

"Jackknife, that's not even…" Bai Long tried to say, only for Luco to raise a hand.

"No. He's done enough," Luco insisted. "I need to keep these burns."

"But… won't dey hurt?" Jackknife asked.

"A bit," Luco assured him. "But we can't remove all the evidence. Rocket might try and plead innocence. Claim she never hurt me."

"Impossible," Diamondback insisted. "I was right there when she did it."

"We both were," Brock said. "You've got an entire town behind you, Luco. No one will deny what Rocket did to you."

"Or what she might do to me now?" Luco asked. "You know she's watching, right?"

Rocket's heart skipped a beat as every eye locked on her. She spun around, ready to go back for Drake. Unfortunately, Diamondback controlled far more than just diamonds.

The trees came to life, seizing and wrapping up Rocket with sharp, wooden fingers. Rocket desperately blasted fire, scorching them away, but a blob of water splashed into her, quenching her flames. Rocket coughed and sputtered, struggling to re-ignite, but in her moment of distraction, a gust of wind threw her backward into a punch from Blaze. The red dragoness hit the ground hard, her limbs vanishing into the soft ground, before the dirt hardened like concrete. Before Rocket could struggle to her feet, Jackknife hit her with another stream of water, and Blaze buried her feet into Rocket's spine.

She didn't even have a chance to scream, as her lungs suddenly emptied of air. In seconds, Rocket was left gasping for breath, soaked, and helpless as the barrel of a firearm pressed into her nape, along with the blade of an axe.

"I would hold still, if I were you," Brock growled.

Rocket wisely ceased her struggles, as the four dragons and their riders surrounded and glared at her. A second later, Luco sauntered into view, back in his regular clothes, though with a new burn scar across the unscathed part of his face.

"Well," Luco noted coyly. "Fancy meeting you again."

Rocket bared her teeth, glowing with flames, only for the click of Tex's firearm to dissuade her.

"DB," Brock rumbled.

Nodding, the earth dragon made a motion with her wrist. The earth rose and entrapped Rocket's snout in a muzzle of clay, barely allowing her room to breathe.

However, as the red fire dragon was restrained, Swift gazed at her with a sad light. "This feels so wrong," he admitted.

Diamondback sighed. "I agree, Swift," she admitted. "We're not supposed to be doing this."

"Not doing what?" Jackknife demanded. "Fighting? Yer bod better dan de fire dragons. You shouldn't let dem make you dink otherwise."

"Jack," Bai Long soothed. "No one's saying that."

"But look!" Jackknife insisted, pointing at Rocket's pinned form. "Who's de best now, huh, Rocky?" He snarled down at her. "Who's...?"

"Aqua-Drake 5436!" Brock boomed, silencing the water dragon.

Luco hushed them, smoothing back Swift's feathers. "I know it's rough," he assured them. "Truly, I do. I wish this didn't have to be this way. Unfortunately, Rocket chose the wrong path."

Rocket growled and pulled her snout up. For a moment, she was able to open her jaws. "All I want is peace!" she protested. "No more death!"

Diamondback hesitated on binding her snout again, before Luco chuckled.

"And that's what we're doing," he said. "Oh, Rocky my friend; Misty is so predictable. She probably told you all about the big bad humans." He knelt down to her level. "But let me ask you something… how many 'bad people' have you actually seen in action? How many humans have you seen lying, cheating, stealing or murdering?"

Rocket's heart hammered in her throat. Despite what Myst told her… Luco was the only one. For each and every other encounter Myst spoke about, Rocket had only seen it through the memories of others.

Luco grinned, before…

"W-What are you talking about?" Swift asked. "What 'bad people?'"

Luco briefly glowered before smoothly transitioning his face into one of sadness. "I'm afraid, my dear dragons, that I haven't been very honest with you."

Rocket's ears perked. Where was he going with this?

"You see," Luco said. "Myst wasn't always… what she is now. Every human the wolves killed? They represented everything that was wrong with this country: pesky, spiteful little children pretending they were 'adults'… believing the world owed them everything because they 'blessed' it with their presence." He scoffed and rolled his eyes. "In a way, Myst is the reason humans are saints now. She killed all the bad ones." His face fell. "Unfortunately, she took it too far. Her job's been done long ago, but she doesn't know when to stop. And that is why all of you are here." He indicated his dragons. "To tell her 'enough.' To let her know her job is done… and to finally put her to rest." He sighed. "Even now, Drake will likely swallow Shiva's lies and deceit of 'peace' and 'cooperation.' He'll let Shiva keep Myst alive, until she can eventually turn someone else. Who's to say she won't try to turn Drake the second he confronts her."

"No," Swift whimpered, before Tex hushed him.

"I'll get 'em before dey get de chance!" Jackknife snarled.

"Jack," Bai Long protested.

Luco grinned. "Good." He motioned for Blaze. "Then let's get them now, eh?"

Jackknife roared in agreement. "C'mon, Li!" he declared. "We got wolves to drown!"

Bai Long didn't look happy about it, locking eyes with an equally nervous Swift. But with Tex already climbing onto Swift, Diamondback pulling up Brock, and Jackknife's water twining around Bai Long's own body, the water dragon rider didn't have much of a choice.

Rocket struggled to pull herself free as Luco's group raced off into the forest, Luco watching them go as he adjusted himself on Blaze's back.

"You can't do this!" Rocket growled. "Drake won't stand for it. He'll order them to stand down!"

Luco's eyes glittered and he jumped off Blaze, getting close to Rocket.

"Well, he's not going to be a problem for much longer," he whispered with a wink.

Rocket's eyes widened in horror, but Luco just turned back to Blaze, who tilted her head.

"Mm?" she asked, pointing at Rocket.

"Nothing you need to worry about," Luco replied, hopping back onto Blaze. "Let's ride!"

Blaze almost looked back, but Luco squeezed her sides, and she was forced to obey, taking to the sky.

"STOP!" Rocket roared. But the dragons didn't look back.

Desperate, Rocket pulled at her restraints, and tried to concentrate. She still knew so little about on the pack link, but she remembered how Myst had managed to contact Shiva even at long range. Rocket had never contacted Myst before. Heck, she didn't even know if it would work.

But she had to try. The wolves had to be warned.

Shiva! Myst! Rocket thought. *Luco's got four of the dragons on his side. He's going to try and kill Shiva and Drake. DON'T GO NEAR HIM!*

So caught up in her thoughts was she, that she almost missed the sound of soft footfalls. She suddenly felt something stab into the dirt, brushing against her scales.

She did her best to turn to the newcomer, only to gasp in hope. "Fawkes?!"

"This is why I don't trust anyone," the bodyguard of Connors growled, digging into the ground. "Just think of what would've happened if I let you and Blaze fly off on your own."

"I'd rather get free of this," Rocket replied.

Shrugging in agreement, the human and dragon worked together, wriggling Rocket's arm free, and from there, the rest of her body.

"Hurry," Fawkes instructed, as Rocket unfurled her wings. "Get Myst and Drake; I'll get Connors!"

Nodding, Rocket took to the air. And all the while she continued to direct her energy and thoughts forward – anything to get Myst's attention.

Chapter 12: Razor's Edge

As Myst sat manacled behind a table in the interrogation room of Cadmus, the urge to break free and race for White Fang Wood was overwhelming. Luco had always been a crafty son of a human. There was no way he was dead.

"Shiva, talk to me," Myst whispered through the link. *"What's the status on the borders of White Fang Wood?"*

"Nothing yet," Shiva said. *"But I saw everything. Jackknife and Swift framing you? Taking Luco away? They've got to have something in store for us."*

"Don't worry," Luke assured both of them. *"We'll handle this. Myst, you and I went through too much to train the demi-wolves in gorilla warfare and archery..."*

Myst sighed. *"That's guerilla, Luke."*

"Whatever it is, we don't need to rely too much on the pack link. Our fighters are ready."

Shiva sighed. *"Then it sounds like we just need to get the mothers and pups to safety. Kodo, can you and your sister handle that?"*

Myst felt Kodo and Celine's presence in the link. *"You want us to flee with the mothers and pups,"* Celine asked incredulously. *"But I can fight."*

"Sister," Kodo protested. *"Mother gave us an order."*

"And that's good for you," Celine refuted. *"But what about Myst. She needs your help too."*

"No," Shiva, Luke and Myst's voices all said as one.

"Celine, while I appreciate the enthusiasm," Myst admitted. *"None of us will be able to focus on Luco if we're worried about you."*

"But you won't have to worry about us," Kodo protested. *"I'm ready, at the very least!"*

Myst sighed. *"Kodo, your time will come. Try to be patient."*

"For once, Myst and I are in agreement," Shiva mused. *"You have your orders, you two. Now get to it."*

"And don't worry about your mother," Luke added. *"I've got her back."*

Myst could feel Kodo and Celine's reluctance through the link. But neither of them said or thought anything. And when Celine tugged at Kodo with a reluctant, *"Let's go, brother,"* he obeyed without further protest.

Unfortunately, while Kodo was seemingly easy to convince, Myst knew that Drake would be a much tougher challenge. As he stormed into the room, his eyes burning with fury, Myst squared herself, took a breath, and prepared for whatever was next.

Just before Drake could speak, however…

"GENERAL!" Rocket's voice cried. "STOP!"

Drake paused, as a crashing sound emanated from outside. Seconds later, Rocket surged into view. Myst was reminded of Shiva's memories; how Rocket had similarly crashed into a cell block looking for Shiva.

But back then, Rocket had been looking for vengeance. Myst prayed that this time would be different.

"Rocket?" Drake demanded. "What in the name of everything sacred…"

"General," Rocket gasped, her chest heaving. "Father… Luco's still alive! He's going to assassinate Shiva… and I think you'll be next!"

Myst gasped, turning back to the link. *"Shiva. Did you hear that?"*

"Loud and clear," Shiva said. *"So, did the pack. We're heading deeper into the forest; Luke and the fighters are ready to stop him."*

"What about you, Myst?" Luke asked. *"We can't leave a pack mate behind."*

Myst wished she could smile at Luke's loyalty. However, when she turned back to Rocket...

"I don't have time for whatever Myst has corrupted you with, Rocket," Drake said. "Get out of here!"

"General, please, this isn't a trick!"

"I gave you specific instructions," Drake boomed. "You were not to harm Luco. Then he comes back burned to a crisp, and then I find Myst finishing the job. Luco was right, Rocket; Buck's death has clearly driven you over the edge."

Rocket stared helplessly at Myst. Myst gripped her manacles, looking down as she felt her own fear mix with Rocket's and even Shiva's.

Shiva! In the pack link, Myst saw a vision! *Blaze and Swift, flying through the air, while Jackknife slithered along the ground, and Diamondback glided along on a floating patch of earth. Bullets flew from Swift's back, and a barrage of fire* tore through the vision.

Myst gasped as she felt the wolf's fear and fury mix and the war begin again. This was what Myst had been afraid of: all she had ever wanted was for her wolves to be safe. And yet, now they were in more danger than ever before. Myst had to stop this.

With strength fueled by desperation and the pack link, she broke her chains like shattering glass. Drake turned to her just as she threw the table at him, throwing him off guard long enough for her to run to Rocket.

"We gotta get out of here, Rocket," Myst said. "He's not going to listen, and we don't have time to make him listen!"

Before Rocket could speak, pink talons closed over her muzzle. A second dragon – this one a bright pink, wrenched Rocket away before Myst could jump onto Rocket's back.

"You may have corrupted this one, Myst," the pink dragon boomed, in a voice that was far from feminine. "But Bang Fifigara is not so easily swayed."

"Bang!" Rocket growled, shoving him. "Get off me!"

Myst paused, unsure whether to take her chances in the hallway or to try and free her dragon. But in that pause, Drake snagged her tail and threw her back into the interrogation room.

"Oh, no," Drake growled. "You're not leaving after all the trouble you caused."

Myst spun, sinking her teeth into his arm. As he released her with a roar of pain, she followed up with several slashes from her claws. But he blocked and kicked her back.

For a moment, human and demi-wolf circled each other.

"I should've finished you in the arena," she growled. "Shiva has too much faith in your kind."

Drake's eyes narrowed as he brought up his fists. "Bring it on, you bitch." He lunged forward with the force of a hurricane, but she had learned from their encounter, and redirected him into the wall.

"Thanks for the compliment," she snarled. "But it won't do you any good."

She went to bite his nape, but...

"Myst, don't!" Rocket cried, too tangled up with Bang to interfere any further.

But her cry did give Myst pause, enough for Drake to elbow the demi-wolf in the gut and spring clear. He swiped at her with his fist, but Myst dodged and scored another cut along Drake's side. Her primal instincts roared in catharsis, wanting her to rend him to pieces.

"Please!" Rocket yelled, wrestling with Bang. "That's my father!"

Myst winced. *He* is *Rocket's father. She loves him. Cares for him.*

As the thoughts of what her draconic partner thought of her opponent overwhelmed her, Myst failed to keep her focus. She snapped back into the fight just as Drake lunged at her again. But though she tried to dodge, his fist still managed to find the bundle of nerves in her spine.

"NO!" Rocket boomed, struggling to throw Bang off.

Myst howled as her entire body froze, yet there was no cold. She tried to move her legs, but it was like an invisible vise had clamped them down. She pitched into the ground, her head throbbing as it crashed against the concrete. Drake stood over her with an expression of pure rage. He caught her wrist when she tried a defensive swipe, and reared his fist back for another blow.

"Drake…" Rocket pleaded, before another voice boomed out.

"GENERAL DRAKE, ENOUGH!"

Drake, Myst, Bang and Rocket all froze, as Connors stormed into view, Fawkes right behind him.

"What is the meaning of this madness?" Connors declared. "Both of you have let anger and hate cloud your minds for the last time."

"Cloud my…" Drake's fist tightened, his knuckles turning white. "King Connors, these wolves betrayed your trust and my dragons! They killed Luco!"

"On the contrary," Connors said, his voice sharp as a knife. "All they did was cook a slab of meat that was put in place of the body."

"Add to that, I saw him," Fawkes added, pointing at Rocket. "We both saw him; gloating to Rocket about how he was going to assassinate Shiva. How he'd try to kill you as well, General Drake."

Drake paused, his fire-colored eyes darting between the two. Myst could see he still didn't want to believe. If even the word of his king wasn't going to convince him...

There is another way, Myst realized. One she hated to consider. But with her pack's lives on the line, and combat no longer an option...

"Luco is playing you for a fool," Connors protested.

"And even if he wasn't," Myst added, "I'm sorry."

Connors and the others paused, turning to Myst as she forced herself into a sitting position.

"I'm sorry," Myst repeated. "For all the pain I caused... all the good people I killed. David... Buck..." She shook her head, kicking herself for disregarding the names of the dead. "I know there's no way I can sponge away the blood on my claws. But please... don't take it out on my pack mates. On Shiva. On Kodo."

Drake blinked, as if not believing Myst was capable of saying such things. "Why?" the General muttered. "Why now? Why... after everything..."

"Because Luco is going to try and kill you and Shiva," Myst insisted. "If Rocket's right – and I have no reason to think she's not," she added with a nod to the dragon, "He's going to try and take control of the dragons from you... and turn the wolves back to the warpath."

"She's right."

Myst, Drake, Connors, and even Rocket stepped back as Myst's fur glowed, and Shiva's voice echoed through. She extended a link to Rocket, and the dragon only paused for a second before taking it. A square image of energy formed before the humans, showing Rocket's memories.

Rocket getting tied down. Luco grinning at her, before turning to the dragons that had joined him.

"Even now, Drake will likely swallow Shiva's lies and deceit of 'peace' and 'cooperation.' He'll let Shiva keep Myst alive, until she can eventually turn someone else."

Bang huffed. "Impossible."

Drake merely shook his head in shock, as the screen flickered – Rocket trying to rise against her bonds.

"You can't do this!" Rocket growled. "Drake won't stand for it. He'll order them to stand down!"

Luco's eyes glittered. "Well, he won't be a problem for much longer," he whispered in her ear.

Drake's fist clenched. "Lies... Slander... he wouldn't..."

"He would and he did," Rocket insisted. "I know how hard it is to escape what we thought, General – believe me, I do. But if we continue to give Luco the benefit of the doubt, he will destroy everything we've tried so hard to protect."

"And what we've tried to protect," Shiva added. "We can stop this madness, but only if we work together."

Drake regarded her, nursing his fist. The demi-wolf held his gaze for one second; two seconds; three. Myst didn't dare test her nerves. Bang was looking to Drake for instructions, and even Rocket and Connors seemed to be waiting for the General's next move.

But Rocket gazed at Drake with pure faith in her eyes. Despite everything, that part of her that still loved and believed in the best of humans was willing to trust Drake to do the right thing.

Hopefully, it wouldn't lead to them both being killed, Myst thought. Because if they died, Shiva died too, and with her, any hope for peace.

For Myst and Rocket, time seemed to slow, each second seemed drawn out. Then Drake finally spoke.

As they approached White Fang Wood, Rocket could hear the roars of the dragons and howls of the wolves rising up from the fight and saw the forest lightning up in shades of yellow and white. The leaf canopy was aflame in places. The wood was now a war zone.

As they drew closer, Rocket saw the battle. Wolves shot back and forth like gray bolts of lightning, dodging around the four dragons as they battled. Swift stayed high in the air, while Tex fired down at the wolves. Another wolf exchanged fire with her, trying to shoot arrows up at Swift, all while he flew higher to avoid them. Jackknife tried to chase the archer wolves out of the trees, soaking them with bursts of water while also trying to defend himself and his rider from being separated by the wolves. Brock attacked with his axe, while Diamondback burrowed into the earth, opening pits up around him and trying to swallow the wolves whole. Yet, the canines' fleet footing allowed most of them to escape Diamondback, and for all his bulk, Brock lacked their speed.

Myst's claws clenched on Rocket's neck. The dragon wondered how Myst felt, seeing her home attacked so brutally.

Above it all, Rocket saw Blaze locked in combat with Luke, fuming in hatred. A few burning arrows still stuck out of her hide, having found their marks, but they didn't slow her down in the slightest.

"MYST KILLED MY RIDER!" Blaze roared, every word forcing Luke back with a fresh burst of flames. "SHIVA! YOU SAID YOU'D CONTROL HER! GET OUT HERE AND FACE ME! I'M GOING TO MAKE YOU PAY FOR ALL HER EVIL!"

Lifting a massive flaming limb that had fallen from a tree, Luke smashed it like a club across the advancing dragon. Chillingly, the blow had no effect.

"You've been lied to, dragon," Luke said. "Sadly, your rider is far from dead."

"LIAR!" Blaze roared, another fireball arcing towards the wolf.

However, a burst of lightning hit the fireball head on, dissipating it into sparks as Shiva stepped into view, her glowing fur unmistakable.

The other dragons momentarily turned, seeing her arrive. Here was their enemy; Luco's words burning in their minds.

Rocket and Myst rolled across the trees on a short final to land in the midst of the battle, Bang carrying Drake right alongside them. As Myst's fur glowed, likely communicating with Shiva, the General's eyes turned down, and caught a glimpse of Luco waiting in the shadows. As Luco moved on Shiva's flank, the General's eyes were round with rage and astonishment.

"He's alive," Rocket heard Drake hiss. "She was telling the truth?!"

Blaze struck before Rocket could respond, the yellow dragon's barrage of flames barely getting absorbed by Shiva's pack link. As Shiva redirected Blaze's flames right back toward her and her fellow dragons, Luco began to rush in. But just before he could blindside Shiva...

"LUCO!" Drake's voice boomed across the clearing.

Rocket grinned at how pale Luco got. All four dragons and their riders froze, stiffening up like children who had been caught by their father, while Bang and Rocket touched down behind them.

Shiva's pack link pulsed as she howled a command, and the wolves stood down.

"Do not attack General Drake!" Shiva ordered.

"All dragons, stand down," Drake barked at the same time.

The wolves and dragons complied... with the exception of Jackknife, who made one last attempt to rush Shiva.

"Jackknife, Drake told us to stop!" Bai Long said.

"No, Li!" Jackknife insisted, struggling against his rider. "I can..."

However, just before the white wolf or her mate could defend, a young, silver-furred juvenile wolf launched out and caught Jackknife with his claws around the water dragon's throat.

"Back off from my mom, shrimp!" Kodo snarled, his own pack link crackling to life.

"SHRIMP!?" Jackknife roared, baring his fangs. "BOY, I SWEAR TO TEETH-FOR-DAYS...!"

"BOTH OF YOU!" Shiva barked. "Stand. Down."

"Jackknife, stop!" Drake ordered.

"You heard them, enough!" Bai Long barked, yanking Jackknife back.

The young wolf and the water dragon winced. But with their leaders glaring down at them, they reluctantly backed up and away from each other, Kodo snarling menacingly while Jackknife hissed angrily.

Luco's assassination attempt had been countered. However, when Drake looked to Luco, Rocket still felt her heart skip a beat at the sorrow and conflict in his eyes.

"Luco," Drake growled. "What are you doing?"

Luco smiled. That cold manipulative smile Rocket remembered him flashing right before he framed her. Before he could speak...

"He's trying to kill you," Rocket said.

"WHAT?!" the dragons boomed.

"Outrageous!" Bang cried.

"Can't be," Dixon added.

"Traitor!" Jackknife and Bai Long insisted.

"We would never...!" Swift agreed.

"Ain't no way!" Tex said.

"That's a bit harsh, don't you think?" Diamondback mused.

Brock and Blaze just growled.

From atop Rocket, Myst called out. "Don't you all see that he's using you; playing on your rage and your anger?" The demi-wolf pointed at Luco. "He wants you all to think the wolves are bad. He wants you to try and kill Shiva so that he can kill Drake and take over. All of this is just his attempt to seize power so he can keep this war going. Just for... stupid, petty reasons that I can barely comprehend!"

"You can't comprehend a lot of things," Luco noted cruelly. "You will always be the enemy, Myst. That's how I designed you." He turned his gaze to the dragons and the General. "My dear General... my friends – human and dragon alike... think of the good you've done stopping them. Think of everyone these wolves have slain." He glared right at Rocket. "Are you saying that Buck doesn't matter to you anymore, Rocky?"

Rocket's eyes narrowed. "You're done manipulating me over my rider." Rocket looked to Shiva. "For too long, I've let my grief and what I was taught blind me to the pain and suffering of those I called my enemies." Her gaze hardened as she glared back at Luco. "But not anymore." She turned back to her fellow dragons. "Drake raised us to believe in honor and fairness. If you follow Luco, you're saying that war is the only thing we're good for. A war based on lies. You're saying you don't want peace. You're saying you're okay with Buck and however many others dying for a pointless conflict that is only fueling the sick fantasies of one human."

Swift backed up, Tex lowering her weapon, while Diamondback and Brock looked at each other in thought. Jackknife was still glowering at Kodo, Bai Long clearly struggling to hold him back, while Kodo eyed Jackknife with disgust. Blaze looked between Rocket and Luco in deep conflict; her sister and her father. Those she loved most in life, now turned against each other.

"It's time to stand down," Rocket said. "This war is over."

"She's right," Shiva said. "If you want to fight, it's won't be because we forced you to." She motioned with her claw, and her wolves backed up with her into the forest. "We will not fight unless you make us."

Rocket planted herself before the forest. "And if you want to hurt them, you'll have to go through me."

Bang gasped. "But Rocket...!" he protested.

"No," Drake said. "She's right. You are supposed to be the defenders of the innocent." Drake grimaced. "King Connors warned me that innocence and humanity are not one and the same." He stood beside Rocket. "It's a mistake that I will not have any of you repeat."

Rocket's spirits soared as she gazed at her General, and he gave her a nod of affirmation.

"Ignis-Drake R065?" Drake said. "You did good."

As Rocket struggled not to grin, she heard Luco groan.

"Well, isn't this a touching scene," he mocked. "Three species of murderers all pretending that they can get along." He laughed darkly, the new scars on his face making him look like a demon.

"That's enough, Luco," Drake said. "You're finished."

Luco's laugh increased. "Oh, my General," Luco mocked. "Before I created the demi-wolves, there was no purpose or meaning to life. And when you enlisted me to create the dragons, to fight the demi-wolves, I gave all your lives meaning! Teeth-For-Days and Reacher? They honor me!"

The dragons straightened.

"Excuse you?" Diamondback demanded.

Luco lifted up a familiar leather bound book. "And you will to."

Shiva tried to grab him with a pack link, but he knocked the tendril aside with an incantation. Ominous red light flashed as he chanted something in a strange language Rocket had never heard before.

Swift yelped, flying higher. "Tex! Do something; s-shoot him!"

"Shoot him? But we were with him!" Tex protested.

"Diamondback!" Brock ordered.

"On it," Diamondback replied, erecting a wall of stone between themselves and Luco.

"Stop him!" Drake ordered.

Blaze stepped backward in confusion, while Jackknife almost went for Kodo again, only for Luke to shoulder check him and for Bai Long to yank him back.

"Jackknife for Teeth-For-Days' sake!" Bai Long cried out.

As the water dragon and wolves nearly began fighting again, Bang and Rocket moved to subdue Luco.

Unfortunately, as Luco summoned a red ball of light, he didn't throw his attack at Drake.

He threw it at Rocket.

Before Rocket could try to dodge, a wall of black fur launched between her and the attack.

Time slowed down as Myst's yellow eyes locked with Rocket's. The wolf was smiling, assuring Rocket that once again, she would protect her.

But as Rocket thought back to all the times Myst had saved her, resolution narrowed her eyes.

Sorry, Myst, she thought. *But this time, it's my turn to save you.*

She grabbed Myst and tucked into a ball, grimacing as the ball of light dug into her back. But Rocket resolved to match whatever happened.

She was a defender of the innocent. This was what she was meant to be doing; protecting others.

With her rider by her side.

Though the other dragons were still hesitant about attacking a human, General Drake had no such restrictions.

Tackling Luco to the ground, he subdued the mad rider with a punch to the throat before kicking the book away from him.

"Grab that book," Drake ordered. "Keep it away from him. Bang, grab him."

Swift stayed in the air, but Diamondback immediately shot through her stone wall and grabbed it, holding it away from Luco and the others. She even glared at Brock when he tried to approach her. Bang, meanwhile, picked up Luco, holding him by the nape with a disturbed look.

"Rocket?" Drake asked, looking around. "ROCKET!" His voice was rising in alarm.

"Myst!

Drake looked back; Shiva was holding a horrified Kodo, while Luke kept himself between the other wolves and the dragons. All eyes were on the smoking crater where Rocket and Myst had been hit.

In their place lay a dragon egg – the size of a football, with a pitch-black surface speckled with spots of gold and white.

"W-What happened to her?" Kodo stammered. "Where's Myst?!"

Drake slowly stepped forward. As did Shiva. When Drake picked up the dragon egg, he felt the thrum of life inside.

Shiva sent her pack link tendrils forward. Gently, they encircled the egg, causing the gold flecks to sparkle

"Are they... inside?" Drake asked.

Shiva grimaced as she read the egg. "It's hard to tell," she said. "I'm not feeling... them. But there's something else. I can't tell for sure."

"We need to break it open!" Luke decided, already stepping forward.

Drake shifted it away from Luke. "No!"

"That might kill whatever's in there," Shiva agreed.

"Plus..." Drake looked over at Diamondback, who was staring at the book with an almost awed light. "That's the book Luco would use to make dragon eggs."

"Is this how he made them?" Kodo demanded. "By… fusing people together?"

Drake shook his head. "No, that's impossible."

"You know that for certain?" Diamondback asked. "You saw him make our eggs?"

"Diamondback, that's enough," Brock warned.

But Drake didn't answer her question. And the implication made Shiva's eyes widened in horror.

"That's how Myst made us," she whispered. "And… didn't she get the book from…"

"Stop," Drake insisted. "We can reverse it."

"Um… General?" Diamondback asked, having already opened the book. "I don't suppose you know how to read any of this."

Drake turned back to her as she held up the book for him. His heart dropped; the book was written in a language he had never even seen before. Strange symbols and pictures were all that adorned the pages. Drake felt his head ache just from looking at the unintelligible scribbles.

Reluctantly, Drake looked to Shiva. But his heart only fell further at the despair and confusion registered on her face.

"I've... never seen anything like that," Shiva mumbled, looking to Drake.

"Neither have I," Drake said. "Which means..."

At that moment, Luco's laugh sounded; a low, ominous chuckle. All eyes turned to the anarchist, as he reveled in their confusion.

Drake marched towards Luco, his grip tightening on the egg. "What did you do to them?"

Luco grinned at Drake. "Out of your depth, General? Don't worry; when one door closes, another opens."

As he continued to laugh, Drake handed the egg to Jackknife, who gently took the egg and held it like a newborn. With his hands free, Drake spun, his fist colliding with Luco's jaw. The world went dark for the former rider.

#

Luco's eyes fluttered open. He found himself shackled in a shadowed cell; the chains anchored to the wall in heavy eyebolts embedded deep into ancient stone. A faint light from the passageway outside filtered through heavy bars in the door, but the light was fighting a losing battle with the darkness.

"Lucas Cooper," a voice said, almost making the rider jump. "It's been some time."

"Connors," Luco chuckled, already imagining the king somewhere in front of him, his black cloak and hood helping him blend into the shadows. He glanced around. "I love the accommodations you got. Top notch."

He could hear the chuckle in Connors' voice. "Only the best for my old friends, Mr. Cooper."

"I appreciate the sentiment, but I go by 'Luco' now."

"Yes-yes," the King mused. "You thought you were so clever; taking the first few words of your name and then combining them into a loose variation of that term for 'crazy.' How original. However, just like how our mutual friend Drake will never be able to not see his dragons as the little hatchlings they started out as, I don't think I'll ever be able to not see you as Lucas Cooper; that poor, lonely little man, so desperate to find meaning in life that he was willing to delve into forbidden occult practices on my behalf, and see what magic he could bring forward."

Luco tensed, the chains straining as he tested their limits.

"And as for this little experiment," the King continued. "Thank everything sacred that it is over." His tone grew cold. "Did you have fun? Did you get everything out of your system?"

Luco chuckled again. "An experiment? That's all this was to you?" He shook his head with a laugh. "And I thought I was cold."

"You can't save the world without a few sacrifices," Connors replied. Luco heard the bolt slide in the door, but the door seemed to move silently on greased hinges. From the darkness, he saw Connors face; his gray eyes glittering with a strange inner light. "Now that we know what that book can do, you and I are going to have no problem uniting this world. But first, we need to ensure that the dragons and wolves don't have any more problems with each other. And that starts with you un-fusing that egg and bringing back Myst and Rocket."

Luco scoffed. "Do it yourself."

Now it was Connors who laughed. "I don't think so. I know what that book did to you; what you had to lose in order to translate its strange wording and letters. I need the others fully functional for the plans that I have in store for them."

Luco leaned back. "Well, looks like we're at an impasse. Because I'm not killing who I made from Myst and Rocket."

Connors' smile didn't fade, even as he slid back into the shadows, the silent door hissing back into its jam. "You will do what I command," Connors replied as the bolt slid home. "How long it takes – and how painful it is for you and those you love – well, that's up to you."

Luco's grin faded. "Painful? I'm…"

"A criminal," Connors cut him off smoothly. "A wanted fugitive, hated for turning the wolves on man, sparking a war and getting thousands killed." He heard a flask unscrew as Connors took a pull. "Who's going to care what happens to you or the ones who helped you?"

#

Drake and Shiva waited in the antechamber beside the throne room – the same room where Connors gave Rocket her mission to catch Luco. Drake paced back and forth, while Shiva sat despondent in the corner, the weight of the silence overwhelming.

She asked, for the third time, "Do you think the King can convince Luco to bring them back?"

The first two times she had asked, Drake had been silent. This third time, he sighed. "Luco... I don't know what to think about him anymore. I hope Connors gets through to him – Rocket's life is on the line as well – but this. Everything Luco's compromised... everything he's done." He ran a hand through his hair. "I was a fool, Shiva. Letting my dragons believe all humans were good."

Shiva's ears flattened. "You just wanted to make sure they didn't hurt the innocent," she said. "You wanted them to be heroes."

"Is Blaze a hero?" Drake asked, looking at Shiva with despair. "Is Jackknife or even Rocket? They did what they thought was right, and now... who knows what the people think?"

"We can show them the truth," Shiva offered. "My pack link can show them."

Drake laughed hollowly. "You showed me the truth," he said. "You showed us all in that arena. And how many of us were willing to believe?"

After a pause...

"Sometimes truth takes time to take hold," Shiva replied.

Drake looked back towards the exit. In his mind, he saw his dragons. His children.

"They call me General," Drake offered, in a strange moment of vulnerability. "But to me, I'll always be their Father. And now I feel like I failed them."

Shiva followed his gaze; in her mind, she saw her mate. Her son. Her daughter.

Shiva paused and reflected. "If parents are doing their job, they feel guilt," she said. "I spend so much time tending to others. Handling pack dilemmas… making sure Myst was safe… that I feel I've neglected my children. Haven't given them the mother they need." She paused. "I'm the one who asked Myst to do this mission." Her voice trailed off. "And now she's gone." She sighed. "Perhaps I failed Myst."

Drake wasn't used to dwelling on softer emotions, but he was drawn to console the demi-wolf. "Try not to think like that," Drake offered. "If Myst is gone, then so is Rocket. And I refuse to believe that."

Shiva nodded. "But for however long Luco stalls… the wolves are going to need an Alpha." She gazed up at Drake. "And the dragons are going to need their General." She lifted herself up.

"It'd be a huge weight off their shoulders if they had one less enemy to fight." She offered her claw.

Drake stared down at her claw, before looking up at her. His expression softened by a fraction, and he took her claw.

"As long as my dragons have one less enemy to fight as well," he said. "It's going to be a challenge showing them what Rocket learned." His eyes narrowed. "I don't need other wolves confusing them even more."

Shiva nodded. "I promise; I'll keep my wolves from your dragons, as long as you can do the same. And we won't bother the humans again. You have my word."

Drake grinned and nodded. "And you have mine." And they shook on it.

The compulsions of good people are too often undone by vanity and petty conceit. And yet fate decrees that even, out of our failures, life finds a way.

In the depths of Cadmus' laboratories, the black egg twitched as the future took hold in the present.

Made in the USA
Las Vegas, NV
21 October 2022